Marley

MORGAN'S LEAP BOOK 4

KATHI S. BARTON

This is a work of fiction. Names, characters, places, and incidents are products of the author's imagination or are used fictitiously and are not to be construed as real. Any resemblance to actual events, locations, organizations, or persons, living or dead, is entirely coincidental.

World Castle Publishing, LLC
Pensacola, Florida
Copyright © Kathi S. Barton 2022
Hardback ISBN: 9798359304061
Paperback ISBN: 9781958336793
eBook ISBN: 9781958336809
First Edition World Castle Publishing, LLC, October 24, 2022
http://www.worldcastlepublishing.com
Cover: Karen Fuller
Editor: Karen Fuller

Prologue

Morgan made herself into a tight ball as she hid herself in the tall grasses in the field. She knew that the men chasing her would find her soon enough. But for now, she was going to make them work for it. Closing her eyes, trying her best to calm her breathing, she did the only thing she knew to do to not think about what was going on around her. Morgan counted to fifty in all the languages that she knew.

She had awakened out here in the tall grass. All

she remembered was having dinner in the kitchen with the staff and then waking out in the middle of the moonless night. She'd not remembered going to bed. Not putting on her night gown she had on now. Nor did she remember waking when brought out here in the cool night. Soon after waking, she heard the voices of the men, six she thought she'd counted, saying that the first one that found her could have her. At fourteen, Morgan knew exactly what that meant. They were going to rape her. Then more than likely, kill her.

Her parents would be looking for her. She would admit, only to herself, that they'd not be too upset about her being gone. Morgan had a habit of getting up in the middle of the night. To see to one creature or another. So it might be days before anyone—

The hot breath of air on her forehead had her whimper just a little. Lifting her head without opening her eyes, she felt it once again. It was hot but not sour smelling. Opening her eyes, she looked right into the golden eyes of a leopard. Their noses touched. That was how close she was to her.

The lick to her face scared her. While she'd seen the wild animals around the compound where she lived, she'd never been this close to one so dangerous. The farmers would kill them when they would take down a cow or something that they raised, but no one could have prepared her for the beauty of them this close.

The big cat put her paw on her head and pushed it back down so that it rested on the dirt. When she started to lift it again, the cat pushed her down again. Understanding that she was to stay where she was, Morgan closed her eyes. If she was going to be eaten, she was glad that the cat was sparing her from knowing when it was coming.

The sound, soft as a coin dropping onto the dusty ground, was all she heard before the large cat screamed. There was gun fire too. Something frighteningly close stirred up some of the dirt she was hiding by. The screaming of men was next. It wasn't long before it was all cut off, and she knew on some level that the cat had killed the men. The paw to her head again had her lifting it up to see if she was next.

The cat had been hurt. Blood was pouring from her shoulder at an alarming rate. Sitting up, unmindful of whether it was safe to do so, Morgan tore at her nightgown to stanch the blood as she spoke to the leopard.

"I think you saved me." The cat just let her poke around at her wound, soon lying down when she asked her to do so. "The bullet needs to come out. If it doesn't, I'm afraid that you'll get sick and die from it. I wish I had my knife here. But I think I can see it enough to get it out with my fingers. I won't do any more than I have to. All right?"

Morgan worked for fifteen minutes on getting the bullet out. The cat never hurt her. Never tried to get away from her as she worked either. Sweat poured off her forehead as she finally got it free. When she was finished, she showed it to the cat.

"See? Someone got a shot in. I promise you; I'll make sure that you're all right. Do you have a lair? Someplace that you can rest?" The cat stood up, and that was when she noticed that she'd had kittens recently. "Oh no. Where are they? You left your den to come to save me? Come on. I'll help you back."

It wasn't far. About a hundred yards from where the cat had come to her. It occurred to her that the cat was more than likely saving her kittens from being found when she killed the men, but Morgan was ever so grateful that she'd spared her as well. Helping the cat into the den, she saw that she had three of the puggiest little kittens she'd ever seen.

"They're beautiful. Oh, look at them. You are a good momma, Golden Eyes. They're very fat. I'll stay with you until you need to eat again. Then I'll hunt for you." The cat didn't seem to mind when she picked one of them up, so she touched each of them in turn. "You're very lucky those men didn't find you too. But I guess you knew that."

She stayed with the family overnight. There wasn't any way she'd be able to make her way back home in the darkness, so it was fine with her to be in the cave for the night. The kittens woke hungry a couple of times in the night. Instead of having

Golden go to them, Morgan carried them back and forth to their mother. She seemed to be all right with her helping that way as well.

When the sun was coming up, Morgan made sure that not only did the family have water, but she also scavenged as much as she could from the horses that the men had come out here in. There was hardtack that was in abundance, but she was also able to get herself some much-needed flint as well as some blankets.

Taking it to the cave, she put the kittens on one of the blankets and then sat down to watch them fall over each other until they had their spot picked out. It was calming to watch them, she thought. They were just too little to do much more than be rolly Polly little kittens.

Giving the hardtack to Golden, she made her way to her home. It was further than she'd thought it might have been, and she didn't arrive there until the sun was nearly down. Going into the house by way of climbing up the back stairs, she heard her parents speaking out their balcony from her own window.

Sliding out onto her own, she stood deeply in the shadows to listen to what they might be saying. Her mother was standing at the railing, her father deeper in the room.

"I cannot believe that she's gone." Morgan started forward, wanting to assure her mother that she hadn't been hurt at all. "This was a brilliant idea that you had, Malcomb. To have it look as if she'd been kidnapped and then killed. I have never wanted anything more than that child dead."

Her heart hurt. Her mind didn't know how this was really what her mother was saying. They weren't close, but she never thought she'd want her dead. But even as her dad came out to the balcony, too, she watched the two of them as they stood there in an embrace.

"Well, it wasn't nearly as hard as I thought it would be to get some men gathered up to take her. As you said, it's a good thing now that she's gone. When they find her body, it will be blamed on anything but me." Mother said that it wouldn't be her fault either. "No. No one will bother with blaming you, my dear.

For all they know, you've committed suicide because your daughter is gone."

It took her less time than it apparently did her mother for what her father was saying. As soon as he pushed her mother nearly over the railing, intending she was sure to make it look as if she had fallen to her death by her own hand, mother grabbed her father's coat.

The two of them hung there for what seemed like forever. Would they both fall? Would they be able to save one another? She didn't care. So when her mother's weight took them both over the edge, Morgan stood there for several minutes thinking about what had just befallen her family. Looking over the edge of her own balcony, she saw them there, tightly embarrassed as if in a lover's hug and dead. Blood spread out beneath their heads as if a bucket of it had been poured over the two of them.

Making her way to the kitchen area, she staggered twice in her grief. Not that they were dead, no, it was that they had planned her demise in such a cold way. Lincoln was there, the butler of the house, when she entered. He took one look at her and sat her in the chair she'd spent more time in than the ones in the formal dining room. Lincoln, she knew, would be her family from now on.

"Child, what is it?" She must have been a mess. Or looked on edge. The slap to her cheek stung enough that she was brought out of whatever thoughts she'd been having. "What's happened? Your parents, they told the household that you'd been kidnapped. Are you hurt?"

She told him everything. Not leaving out anything, including the cat that had saved her. Also, leaving no doubt to the older man that her parents had planned for her to be killed this night. Lincoln sat down across from her after making her a cup of tea that was mostly bourbon.

"You are mistress of the house now. Tomorrow we will find their bodies whilst you are still abed. You will say that you were out with the creatures of the field. They will believe that well enough. That is where you are most of the time." She asked him about the cats. "'Tis your decision. However, if you were to bring them here, none of the rest of the staff will mind. It is you we stayed for all these years and not your parents."

"I'll need help bringing them here." He said that he'd go with her. "They're far. Much further than I had thought. But I wish them to be safe, Lincoln. She saved my life, and I will do the same for her and her family."

"You have a good heart, child. A very good one. We shall leave now and take lanterns with us. A basket, too, so that we might carry the little beasts." She sked him if he didn't want them here. "Nay, I want what you want. We all do. Tomorrow after your parents are found, we'll be as we should have been. A good home and a safe one. Mark my words on that. I will talk to you as we go about now that you are mistress of the house what men will do to get to you. They'll want you, but you're too stubborn to be a good wife to anyone seeking your hand. It might be well that there are cats here to protect you. You have become a very wealthy woman."

As they were making their way to the cave, she

wondered if he knew how safe the house would be with leopards in it once. Once the kittens grew up, they'd be as big as she was now. Smiling, she thought perhaps she wasn't all that upset about her parents being dead. They'd been treating her as if she had for as long as she could remember.

Golden seemed happy to see her. She licked her face and brushed her with her large paws. As Lincoln gathered up the kittens, she helped Golden outside to do her business. It took a great deal out of her, and Morgan had to carry her back into the cave. Once they were all loaded up in the buggy, she sat down with Golden to tell her what had happened.

"So I'm motherless except for you. I know that you're a cat and I'm only a human, but I think we can get along. When the men start to come, and according to Lincoln, they will, I'll need you to protect me too. I shant ever marry. Not only that, but I'm also going to make it my life's work to make sure that animals such as yourself are as safe as I can make them."

Arriving home well after the sun had settled in the sky again, she made sure that the mother and kittens were safe in her parent's big bed. There was a fire in the fireplace for them should the night turn too cold. Morgan also made sure too that the mother had plenty to eat, having given her one of the steaks that her father would treat himself to daily while she had whatever else he had with his meal.

Sleep didn't take its time capturing her, luring her to a night's rest. It hit her right between the eyes and had her nearly sick with exhaustion. As she closed her eyes, sleeping in her own bed as if nothing had happened, she knew that she'd keep her promises to not just Lincoln and the other staff but to herself as well. The animals here would need her, and she was going to make sure they were as safe as they could be while she was still living.

~*~

Four years later

Morgan watched the man as he ran out of her home. How he'd gotten in was beyond her, but now that he was gone with a little less of his fancy clothing, she sat down on the front veranda and waited for the cats to come to her. Over the last month or so, men had been showing up at the oddest times to tell her that she must marry them.

They would all come around sooner rather than later. All of her leopards, as well as a plethora of other such creatures, would come to make sure that she'd not been harmed or taken away from them. None of them would be harmed here, and daily another one or two would come limping into the compound and be welcomed. Golden came to sit at her feet, and she smiled at her when she looked at her.

"He had it coming. We both know that. The pompous ass thought that if he could tear at my clothing, I'd allow him to marry me so that I'd be happy. He said that I'd need someone like him to watch over my money and keep me from dying an old spinster. Apparently, women aren't meant to think beyond having a man around. I'm much happier without him, I think. What did he think I'd been doing here all alone since my parents were dead? Waiting on someone to recuse me? Not likely." Morgan slid to the floor and put Goldens head on her lap. Running her hand down the length of the cat, she could feel her newest litter wiggling around. "I am worried about you, mistress cat. You're heavier this time with your brood. Not to mention, I know that the wound you suffered for me so long ago bothers you more daily. The babes that you brought here that night, they have gone on to have their own children. I cannot believe that so much time has passed since that night." She thought of something and put her forehead to Goldens. "I just realized that you're a grandmother. Congratulations."

"That would make you an Aunt in her eyes." Morgan reached for her gun, something she'd been carrying since that night and found it gone. "You cannot kill me, mistress, but I would prefer that you not harm me either. I have come to speak with you about the good works you are doing here. The one you call Golden; she has asked me to come to speak to you about a great many things. In addition, I have some things I need to ask of you too."

"Who are you?" The beautiful woman asked if she could tell her in a moment. "So long as you know that whatever it is you're hawking, I want no part of.

We're doing very well here on our own."

"You are doing better than well, I think. The ground is fertile here, thanks to your way of doing things. Not all humans would leave an animal to rot on their land without doing something with it." Morgan told her that other animals took care of it. "They have indeed. Even the things that the larger breeds cannot eat or use, the smaller creatures come to salvage what they can use. You have a good system here. A system that will not be something popular for a great many years."

"I don't want to have to go into town." The woman nodded, her smile something that she thought was more than beautiful. "You said that you came here because of Golden. She is a cat. How is that possible that she would call to you?"

"Let me start at the beginning, please. The night that your parents died, the night that you came to help Golden, it was thought that you should have died along with them. Sometimes, with humans, the apple does not fall far from the tree. But you are nothing like them, are you, sweet child. You were not only different than them, but a kinder, gentler person than any of us have ever seen before. We have all been watching you these last years." Morgan asked her who *they* were. "Ah, that brings me to your first question. I am Tellus, the terrestrial being that cares for and is wholly a part of the earth. The earth and the land that you have here. Not for my doing but your own. This land is rich beyond anything man has ever seen before."

Morgan didn't speak, letting all that the woman told her to settle into her mind. She'd been alone for most of her life now and had learned not to prattle on when there was no one to talk back to her. Petting Golden, she was glad to hear her purring. The rumbling of her throat was soothing to her for some reason.

"Mother earth. I've read about you. You're Roman." She said that was correct. "All right. So you're here because I have good land. However, I still don't know why you took time out of your what I'm sure is a busy day to tell me that."

"You are a jewel among all the stars in the sky,

Morgan." Confused at the words and their meaning, Morgan continued to pet her cat. "We, the other earth creatures, have been watching what you were doing here since that night. We've not had to once intervene in helping you care for the animals, all that you protect here. You have lifted a great burden from all of us. Even creatures that you may not be yet aware of have found a home here among the others and have been safe from harm. One such creature sits there on your leg. His name is Button."

Morgan looked down at her leg and saw the tiny creature standing there. She put out her free hand, and when he hopped upon it, she brought him closer to her face. Yes, he was a little man, just like the men that had been coming around but for his size. Then while she was watching him closely, he spread out his wings and fluttered above her palm for several seconds before settling down again.

"Faerie." He bowed before her. "I have read of such creatures as this one. They are thought to be a myth. Such as you are, Lady Earth. I have either hit my head, or I'm being visited by creatures that are as magical as the sun coming up and then resting in the other sky."

"You are seeing magic, my child." Nodding, she laid her hand back on her leg. Button didn't sit on her leg again but stayed on her palm. "He wishes to be with you. To help you in the coming years. For as much as I'd like to say your life will be filled with only riches, we both know it is never that way."

"Nay, it is not. The banker says I owe him great funds for a loan that my parents took out before they died. Also, I have a man who is trying his best to catch me unawares so that he might rape me to take my lands. I don't think he means to keep me around much longer than it is for me to say, 'I do.' They only want what I have." Tellus said that she could help her with those things. "Thank you, my lady. But I'm sure you have enough to do now with the earth as large as it is."

"I do. But helping you is not something that I take lightly, my child. We all, all the creatures in charge of the parts of the earth you now own, are happy to help you. And in doing so, they will get the help they need as well." Morgan asked her what they wanted her to do. "You will do it, will you not. Even not knowing what it is that we ask of you."

"I will help the earth for as much as it gives back to us here. And that, as you know, is a great deal. We are self-sufficient here. Water is ours to use as we see fit. There is a roof over our heads when necessary. The fields, as you have pointed out, are rich and give us back so much more than we can eat. I share what I cannot have put up or preserved." Tellus told her that she knew that as well. "If you need for me to do more, I will do it to the best of my ability."

"Thank you." Tellus looked at her, then at Golden as she continued. "Golden will stay with you until the kittens are born. Her children will be the first of many creatures that will take on this new magic that we wish you to help with."

"She's going to die." Tellus nodded but didn't look at her. "I thought when I've seen her around this time, she wouldn't make it for long after. You do know that she's the only friend that I have besides the people that work here? I've spent long hours thinking about how I will make it without her counsel. Without her snuggling up to me when I need it. I don't know that I want to. But I must, for the others."

"Yes, you will." Tellus told her of the magic that would be given to her. About the babes that Golden would have and how they would go on to be great men. To help her in ways that Tellus and the others hadn't thought of yet. "The magic they will get will help them to be a part of the world of men. To breach such places that, even now, frightens us a little. We will need you to help them blend into such places. To walk, talk and to act like real men. The abilities that we will give to them will make them a prize should anyone find out. So it is important that they do not give themselves away while men. Do you understand?"

"Yes. I'm to be their teacher." Tellus told her, too, that she would be their mother. "I have questions now, but I know that I will have so many more when the time comes. I will teach them everything that I can. Give them whatever step up they'll need so long as I live. I promise you they will be the best of men too. Not like the ones that come here sniffing out an easy way to my home."

"You will not die either, Morgan. You will be around for their children to come into the world, as well as all the shifters that are to be born." Morgan asked her about the men coming around. "They will not come around again should you wish it. Button will have for himself to use an army of faeries that will come to your aid in that and anything else you might need them for. Do not be fearful of using them either. Rightly so, they are excited to serve one such as yourself. You have been titled with the name Queen of Shifters."

"You don't have to do that, my lady. I said that I would help you." Tellus laughed, and it made Morgan smile. "I will do as asked. The rest, I will accept it as part of my duties, but I don't see myself using it overly much."

"I foresee you using the magic given to you much more than you think you will." Tellus laughed again, bringing yet another smile to her face. "I will also give you a list of things that you will need to invest in. They will fund you better than a bank will, and you will remain self-reliant at the same time. Also, the bank has been taken care of. He will no longer bother you about funds he thinks you owe him."

"Thank you for that." Morgan looked down at her friend and ally in all this. "What will become of me when you no longer have a use for me, my lady?"

"There will always be a use for you, child. A creature such as you will forever bond with the earth and make everything around you a better place. I have such faith in you." Morgan told her that she could only do her best. "And that, my child, is all that I could ask for."

The two of them talked throughout the morning and into the evening. Ending up in the living room where there was a fire roaring in the hearth, they were served their tea there as well as juice too. She was told, too, that she'd need to be drinking a great deal more of the elixir. And that the fresher it was, the better it would be for her after using magic.

At some point, Tellus took her hand into hers and gave her the magic she'd need. The power of it washed over her in waves. So much so that for several minutes she had to sit still in her seat and wait for it to settle out. Not only did she receive the magic, but the knowledge of how to use it. Also, things, as she'd been told that she must invest in. Things that Tellus told her that would be worth a great deal in the future.

After Tellus left her to rest, she was told, Morgan sat in the yard at the back of her house. Lincoln came to sit with her a spell, telling her that there were faeries in the kitchen now that would make sure that the household was safe. Also, he said, he'd been given magic as well.

"It is to keep the house in order. To build out when you need it, my lady." She said that she'd been told she'd need to have a larger house. "I find that hard to believe, but I will do what it takes to have you safe."

"I now have more land as well. Tellus told me that there are now five thousand acres here that will be used for the animals in need. No one will be able to enter the land if they wish to harm anything that calls this place home. What am I to do with all this knowledge and wealth, Lincoln? I know I'm to teach the next generation of cats born to Golden, but how much do you think they'll need from me? What am I to do when they go out and have their own leap? I shall be an old woman with only you to keep me company." He asked her if he was immortal as well. "You are. But I was told that at any time you wished to die, I could take it from you. No harm will come to you with it either."

"I think I shall stay with you, my lady. I think we will need each other in the coming years, don't you think?" She said that she needed him every day. "You are so kind to me, Morgan, that I wonder at times why your parents wanted you dead."

"They were in love with themselves." She knew that to be true as soon as she said it. Looking at the older man, she smiled at him. "You and I will do the best we can and hope that it's right. Someday, I think we'll look back on this and wonder what all the fuss was about. Don't you?"

"I think I will hold my thoughts on that until such time as it comes to an end." He laughed a little. "Do you believe it will come to an end, my lady?"

"No. I don't. I don't have any idea why but I think we're going to be having something new and something strange happening as a daily routine." She stood up when he did. "Let us begin this new phase of our life, Lincoln, and hope that we make it work better than the thoughts in my head are making it. All right?"

"Whatever you wish, my lady. We will do well together, I believe." She hoped so. It seemed like a great deal was depending on her doing just that. Making it work for the safety of all involved. She only hoped that she knew enough and was strong enough to make it work for all of them.

~*~

Many, many centuries later

Sin fell in love with the little town again. She'd loved it here as a child, growing up in a place that hadn't been updated since before her mother had been born. The place looked the same, but it was also different, she realized. There were more people walking around than she remembered ever seeing before and a group of kids playing on the swing set in the middle of town. Sin had wanted a swing in the worst sort of way when she'd been a child.

The place where she'd been told to meet Morgan was just outside of town. The large shop was doing a good business, and it looked like everyone was coming out of the place as happy as she'd ever seen them. Once she had pulled into a parking spot in the back of the shop, Sin made her way to the front door, stopping to look at the well-maintained gardens and flowers around it.

"You must be Sin." She nodded at the man standing there with the door open. "My wife is Zippy. I'm Bailey. We spoke on the phone."

She couldn't help herself. Sin hugged Bailey. She'd been thinking about how these people, without thought to themselves, had saved her from driving into a truck and keeping her little brother out of harm's way. When he invited her into the place, she was introduced to the women behind the counter.

"Hello, Morgan. I'm so happy to see that you're doing well." Sin hugged Morgan, too, knowing this woman was the sole reason she was still alive. "I've thought of nothing else for the last few hours except how you would keep me fed and warm when I was a child. I don't have any idea how you knew I needed you, but you were always there. For me."

"Yes. And you've turned out all right yourself, haven't you? Good for you. Your brother, Cody, reminds me a great deal of you when you were his age. While he's not as outspoken as you could be, he certainly makes his point well enough. How are you really, Sin?" Nodding, she followed her to the back of the store and sat at the table there. "I've been in contact, so to speak, with your mother. There are a couple of things you need to know before Cody gets here. She's not going to be coming back here to get him. She had managed to get herself in some deep trouble yesterday, and she's in jail. They found several playing cards on her when they arrested her. She'd been cheating."

"That sounds like something she'd do. How much is she down in gambling? I'm sure it's not a paltry sum." Morgan told her. "How the hell did she manage to talk someone into letting her bid that much on a game?"

"I might have had something to do with that. Melody has harmed you and Cody enough, and I don't want her around anymore. This way was better than what Bailey wanted to do with her. He wanted to hang her out to dry." Sin told her she'd tried that once before, getting dry. "Yes, I heard about that. But this way, you can say you tried, and no one will think any less of you. Not that I believe you care what people think about you and your relationship with her, but you never know about people."

"That's very true. What else is there? You said a couple of things." She told her about the house and how it had been condemned. "That should have happened when I was living there. I'm sure it's not improved with age."

"No, it hadn't. Also, you should be aware that Cody has a little magic. I would imagine you do as well since you've arrived. He can and is glad to be able to have any kind of clothing he wants to wear. He's been playing around with it and has discovered he doesn't want to go back to wearing anything that isn't his in the first place." They both laughed. "He has missed you. Cody has been telling us about how you would call him every day after he'd gone to bed to make sure he was all right. That was, I think, the only thing that kept him going while living with your mom."

"I wanted to bring him with me when I left the last time. I was even going to just take him. But she said I'd never make it out of town with him before I was arrested. Then she told me she'd make it, so I never saw him again. In a permanent way. I was afraid for Cody, but I left him." Morgan told her that was probably the best she could have done. "I don't know. Even now, I hate that I had to leave him behind." Sin heard a man's voice in the shop and had to laugh when he was taken to task by one of the other women out there. "Your son, I'm guessing?"

"Yes, Marley. He's just closed up his practice

today, and he's feeling a little wild. You should meet him." Everything in her froze. "Sin? What is it?"

"I don't know. I mean, until you suggested meeting him, I had no desire at all to meet anyone new. Now I have this insane need to go out there and let him hold me." Marley came to the doorway where they were sitting. "Hello?"

"Hello to you too. Mom, Cody is with me. I didn't tell him that his sister was here until I made sure she was. He's been hanging out with me while the kittens were being born." Marley kept looking at her, then at his mom. "Why do I feel like I've just interrupted something?"

"You didn't. Come here, Marley. Tell me if Sin is your mate."

Before he could move to do that, even if that had been his plan, Cody came rushing into the room and grabbed her. Morgan left her there with her brother when Marley sat where his mom had been sitting.

"Sin, I'm so glad you're here." Cody went on about how he'd watched kittens being born. How he could change his clothing and now had his own bed in the big house. Sin didn't pay any attention to him and was shocked when he snapped his fingers in front of her face. "You're zoned out. Are you all right?"

"Yes. I'm just fine. And I heard you. Sort of." She hugged him again, tickling him until he called for mercy. When he left them to go help out front, she looked at Marley. "You're him. My mate, aren't you?"

"I am yours, yes." She asked him what that meant. "It means that I belong to you forever. You're very beautiful, aren't you?"

"I don't know about that, but I don't look like a hag." He laughed, and Sin joined him. "I'm not sure why I feel all right with this. I've been keeping men at a distance my entire life. However, with you here, I feel as if I'm settled. That my life has a purpose again. Or something like that. Am I making any sense?"

"Yes. I feel that way as well. Like I've been waiting for this moment all my life, and now that you've found me, I can rest easy." He took her hand into his, and she felt a strange and powerful connection. "You've got magic now. And you're an immortal. So is Cody. He's a wonderful little boy. I'm sure you had a great deal to do with that."

"He's going to need me." Marley nodded and said he'd do whatever was necessary to keep them both safe. "It's more than that. I don't want him to be pushed aside ever again. I need to make sure he's better off than I ever was."

"Of course you do. And I'll help you with that. The two of you are my priority from now on. I will bend mountains to make sure no harm comes to either of you again." It was too easy, this thing between them. But she really couldn't find any fault with it. Like she wanted to be mad at him for being so nice about this, but she was happy. "You're thinking very hard. Is there anything I can help you with?"

"I have so many thoughts in my head right now that I'm not sure how to make any sense of it all." Marley didn't tell her he understood but continued to hold her hand. "Are you always going to be this...I don't know, giving of yourself? While I can use it on occasion, I might need for you to get a little upset at me sometimes."

He laughed, and it brought a smile to her face. As they sat there, not really talking about much of anything, Sin realized that just that quickly, she'd fallen in love with the big man. She couldn't find anything wrong with falling so quickly, but it did frighten her just a little.

When the shop closed up, they all walked to the house. She was able to leave her car in the parking lot behind the place and enjoyed the freedom of walking in the cool crisp evening. Once they were at the house, she was shown around. The place was much larger than it looked like from the outside.

"Magic." Sin asked Hanna if they all had magic. "We do. I've been able to get a great deal from a family of unicorns. Veni and Zippy are witches, Veni being the grand witch. Morgan, as you know, has been gifted more than anyone with her magic. Just so she could help the creatures she cares for."

"What about the others? Allison?" She told her what had transpired recently. "A phoenix? I don't know that I ever thought they were real. I'm assuming there are a great many things that people think aren't real that are living here."

"You'd be right on that." They were called to dinner then, and she followed the others into the largest dining room she'd ever seen. "You'll need a faerie too. Cody has one already, but you'll need one to help you out with the magic. After you get it, you'll be able to hang out with him and have him do errands for you."

"A faerie." They all laughed, and she wasn't sure if they were telling her the truth or not. Then, just as she was picking up her fork to have a bite of her dinner, a little person, no bigger than a lighter, sat on the end of her fork. "You're real."

"I am, mistress. My goodness, but you're glowing with happiness." She thanked him and then looked around. "You're going to be very happy here, I'm thinking. You and Marley are a good pairing. I'm glad to see that he's going to be all right after what the other women did to him."

As he explained what had happened with

Piper and her mother, Sin was beginning to see that this family was one to be with. They cared for each other, and they loved with all their hearts. Marley asked her if she was all right.

"Yes. I do think I am. I'm actually better than all right, to be honest with you." He took her hand into his and kissed the back of it. "You're a nice man, aren't you, Marley? All of you are nice."

"Thank you. We had a good role model in our mom. She's worked hard all her life to make us the men we have become. And any one of us would die for her if it ever came to that." Sin told him she could see that. "Thank you again. I'm thinking we're going to get along just fine, aren't you?"

"I am. I might even manage to not make you pissy with me just to see your temper." He said he didn't have one. He was the most laid-back person in the family. "Good to know. You've just challenged me to see what I can do to get your self-control out of whack."

It was perhaps the easiest evening she'd ever spent with strangers. Not that they were that for long, but it was nice to be able to sit around and talk about anything under the sun and not have to worry about impressing anyone. Not that she did that all that much. Sin liked to think she was her own woman. But this, being with this family, was something she'd never had as a child nor as an adult.

She must have dozed off because when she woke up, she was in a large bed. The room was huge, with a large fireplace across the room. Getting up, not even sure what time it was, she headed to the bathroom en suite. Taking a long and warm shower, she felt as if she could face the day a good deal better. Going to the kitchen, Sin realized she had slept past her normal time, and it was coming up on lunchtime. Morgan was playing with one of the kids while she made pies.

"My name is Sammy. You must be Sin." She said she was. "Cody is in my room getting a couple of books he wants to read. I'm going to help him with his homework when we get him to school. You want him to go to the school we go to, don't you?"

"I don't know anything about that school. Nor

do I know what I'm doing right now." He said he'd help her figure it out. While she was drinking a glass of juice, a gnome, an honest-to-goodness gnome, peeked his head out of Sammy's pocket. "Is that for real?"

"Yes. His name is Thad. He's the king of all gnomes. He's my best friend in the whole world." Sammy took the little man out of his pocket and put him on the table beside her. "He's going to retire, and he wants me to take over his job. I'm not sure how good I'll be at it, but I'm going to give it my best shot."

"I see." She looked at Morgan, wondering if she was still asleep and dreaming this. Sammy took her hand and put a crystal on her palm. "Oh my, that's beautiful. Where did you get it?"

"These are all over the place around here. I got that one when I had my birthday last week. It's for college if I want to go. Grandma Morgan said I could buy a college if I wanted to with that. I don't know that I'd want an entire college, but it's good to know I have options." She laughed, then covered it with a cough when Sammy looked at her oddly. "You're overwhelmed, aren't you?"

"Yes. By a great deal, as a matter of fact. I don't suppose I could ask you to tell me things like that a little at a time, could you?" He said he could do that. Cody joined them with several books that looked like first editions of ones she'd read as a child. "I used to love these stories when the teacher read them to us in school. I've not thought of the *Stinky Cheeseman* in years."

As Cody read the story to her, she enjoyed her lunch. Morgan had made nine pies by the time the boys were ready to go out of doors, and she helped her pack them up to give away. She asked her about that.

"Oh, we have fruit here year-round. So when I have a little extra, I try to make sure I give them to people who might enjoy them as much as I do making them. You should take a walk around to see what you can get into. I'm going to be going over to the seedlings here when these are finished. If you'd like, you can hang out with me."

"I'd love that." And Sin knew she would, too. Marley had been called away, she'd been told, to see to a patient that fell at their home. While hanging out with Morgan, she learned a great deal more about where she would be living. Sin had no illusions that she'd not be living here with the rest of the family. It was the way it was meant to be, she thought.

Chapter 1

Sammy had found out that his best friend in the whole wide world was going to die. As soon as he became the new king of gnomes, Thad was going to die and leave him all alone. When his grandma Morgan sat down beside him, he didn't bother looking at her. He was, if he was honest, ashamed of the tears that he'd been shedding.

"When I was just a little girl, my parents decided that I'd be better off going away to boarding school. I wish they would have sent me away. However, I might not have been who I am today if they had." He said that he didn't want to talk today. "I'm talking, not you. So hush up and listen to me. Anyway, when they found out that it would cost them a great deal of money for me to be away from them, they kept me at home. I got my education from the servants, my dearest and best friends in the world. They taught me how to read, write and do math. My parents only wanted me away from them, so I had plenty of time to—"

"He's going to die." Grandma Morgan nodded and asked him if he thought that everything lived forever. "No. I mean, I guess we will, but that's not fair that he's going to leave me, and I'll have no one to hang around with."

"I don't care for pitiful children, Sammy. You, of all people, should know that by now." He looked away and wiped at the tears. He was angry with her for not being there for him. "As I was saying, I learned a great deal from them. Not just how to be a good person, though anything would have been better than they were, but to learn how to care for the very hand that fed us. The earth and all the creatures."

"Thad taught me all that too." Grandma Morgan said nothing for a few minutes, and he looked at her. "Your mom and dad were worse than mine were, huh?"

"Yes. They were going to have me killed simply because they had no use for me. But they were no better than anyone else that comes around thinking that they're way is the best way." Sammy watched the faeries as they rode the goats around the yard. "No one knows this but you, Sammy. I wanted to kill myself too. When Golden left me. I didn't want to raise her children to be better men. I wanted her friendship. Her love and support. At the time, I thought that she had tasked me with too much. A mere slip of a girl raising six cats to become men she could be proud of. She trusted me, above all others, to do what was necessary to make the world a better place, and I sometimes feel that I failed her. Back then, and even sometimes today, I'm not even proud of myself."

"But you did such a wonderful job." She

nodded and told him that it didn't mean that she wasn't heartbroken. "I get it. You're saying that even though Thad is my best friend in the world, that he's given me a great gift in not just taking over his job but that he trusted me to do it."

"No. But that's a good point. However, what I'm telling you is that you're much stronger than you think you are. Smarter too. And of all the gnomes in the world, he chose you to take on his duties when he could have just left it to some other gnome that didn't care as much as you do about the earth and its creatures." He looked up at his grandma, tears still threatening to fall. "Even though Golden has been gone for more years than I can count, I miss her as much as I did back then. When she took her last breath, Sammy, I felt as if it were mine too."

He sat there for a long time before he realized that his grandma had left him. When Thad sat down beside him, just sitting on the step and not saying a word, Sammy realized that this was something else that he loved about the elderly gnome. He didn't need to bother him with talking when he was thinking.

And Sammy was thinking very hard.

"Those goats are gonna wish they'd never seen a faerie before if you ask me." He watched as the faeries took turns riding the goats to guide them to the areas that needed the most trimming. "They're giving the ground a great deal of fertilizer too. Never would have thought to have a double working animal like they are."

"I'm going to miss you, Thad. So much that my heart hurts with it." Thad told him that his heart was hurting, too, when he thought of not seeing him again. "I'm going to do you proud. I might make a whole lot of mistakes, but I'm going to start all my projects with the thought of making you proud of me."

"I'd rather you would think that you're making yourself proud of you, young man. Sammy, you're going to be a better king than I am." Sammy asked him how that was possible. He wasn't even a gnome. "Well, I'll tell you. You've been around a little bit compared to me, but you've seen things that I'm only just realizing that are out there. Being an old gnome, I've been lazy in figuring out things. I'll only admit that to you. But I have been. I had me a way of making things work, and that's the way I did it. Forever. I never thought of changing things like you telling me about the water for the seeds. I knew that the faeries were carrying that water to them one little bucket at a time, but that's the way we'd been doing it for centuries. It just never occurred to me that there might be an easier and better way of doing things. Also, I don't know if you're aware of this or not, but some of them faeries have been singing your praises since you took a big work load off their shoulders. Then there is the way you figured out the fan system in the greenhouse. I never would have thought about having one of them solar panels put up. Lady Morgan, she was as tickled as peas when you showed her how it was going to make the rooms cooler when it was hot out. Too hot, I'm thinking now for the little ones to be working the earth. She's been getting them for other places too. I never in my wildest dreams would have ever thought of solar panels. Much less how they work."

Sammy smiled at his friend. "You would have thought of it sooner or later." Thad told him that he'd not. He hadn't any idea that they were even such a thing. "Don't dumb yourself down, Thad. You're a brilliant gnome and have been taking care of things for a very long time. I'll never be the gnome that you are."

"I hope you won't be." Sammy asked him what he meant. "Young man, this world is changing every single minute. I was stuck so far in the past that it never occurred to me to look up things on one of those computers things. I would have just kept going on and on without thinking beyond where I was now. You took me out of that rut and got this place on the right track. You're going to make the world a better place because you're not thinking things are all right the way they are on account of them working. No, you see something, and you get it working better. I'm right proud of you, son. In fact, I don't think I've been more proud of someone in my whole life than I am of you."

Again the two of them sat there. The yard was

looking better. Even with the dusting of snow that was on the ground, he would see where improvements were being made. The goats weren't to eat the herbs or the small trees. Thankfully the faeries were there with them to make sure that they didn't. Come spring, with all the poop on the ground from their droppings, he'd bet the yard would be as pretty as the gardens that Grandma Morgan had.

"Are you going to take the job, Sammy?" He looked over at Wendy, his sister, when she spoke to him. "Mr. Weeds left a bit ago. I thought you might be getting cold, so I came out to see if I could sit by you to warm you up. So, are you?"

"Yes. I think so." She told him that he needed to decide yes or no. "I know that, but I'm worried that I'll mess it up, and people will be upset with me."

"How long have we lived here?" He told her a few months. "Right. And in all that time, has anyone ever said to you that you're a screwup?"

"I don't think they'd be that mean to me about it, but no, they've not. Not like Rebecca did all the time. Why?" She told him what she thought. "Okay,

I guess I can see that. When I mess up, I just start all over and try again. But this is about the whole world."

"And? Do you think that anyone here hasn't messed up sometime? That Grandma Morgan didn't mess up once in a while when she was bringing up our dad?" Sammy said that he'd never seen her mess up. She was perfect, as far as he could tell. "You're a dummy. Of course, you've not seen her mess up. Do you know why? Because she starts over and learns from her mistakes. The same as you do when you're working. No body is perfect. Not Grandma Morgan. Not even Mr. Weeds. Not you, for sure. So what? You mess up? Will the world end if you make a small mistake and not learn anything from it? Not hardly. It's like me helping with the auction house. I was only there to take notes, but I could see that there would be more sales and more people coming in if the place was more welcoming. I made a lot of mistakes when I was taking notes. Like I thought that they should just let everyone in to bid on things. I was told that wouldn't work because a lot of people don't have the money to go into a place like the auction house where we were and bid on things. Not the kind of prices that sell in a place like that. Just because they've been to a couple of house auctions doesn't mean that they have all the ins and outs of buying things."

"You know, if people that didn't have much money knew how much those things in that place were worth, it would be a robbery every minute." Wendy told him there was that too. "You think I can do this job for the world?"

"I think that if you think you can, Sammy, you can do whatever you want to do. All of us can. Especially with parents like we have now. If not, then why are we even here? Trying to better ourselves more than we were before? You know what? I was just thinking that if anyone could do this, rule the gnomes, it would be you. You're my little brother, and I believe in you like nobody else in the world." He thanked her. "No need for that. But I believe in you, Sammy. The same way that I hope you believe in me."

"I do. I believe in you because you're smart."

She told him that he was as well. "I don't feel that way sometimes. Sometimes I feel like a big dummy that—ouch." She pinched him. "What was that for?"

"For being a big dummy head. You can do this. I know you can, and more importantly, Mr. Weeds does. I know you're going to miss him. I will too. The world will. But with you there, helping them do the things that are needed, doing things that he didn't, the world will be a much better place than I think Mr. Weeds ever thought it would be." Sammy didn't ask her how she figured that.

Sometimes Wendy could be a bit on the painful side when she thought you weren't paying enough attention to what she was telling you. Instead, he thought of all the things that he'd already done for the world. The projects that he was working on now. And even though he'd not done a great deal of the things that he had in his head, he thought for sure that Wendy was right. He did need to take the job.

For the rest of the afternoon, Sammy walked around his yard. Grandma Morgan joined him twice. Once when she was going to the barn to milk the cows, and the second time when she was looking for someone to taste her jelly. That was a job that he enjoyed more than anything else in the world. She made some of the best jellies that he'd ever tasted.

He saw Marley a couple of times too. The woman he was with seemed all right, but she was kind of scary. Every time she thought that her brother was in over his head, she'd scream at him to get down or stop what he was doing. It wasn't until Aunt Veri showed up that Sin began to calm down. Sammy asked his aunt what was wrong with Sin.

"She's worried that if her brother gets hurt that the courts won't let her raise him. She's going a bit overboard being afraid for him." Sammy told her that was just silly. "Perhaps to you. But to her, it's a natural reaction to wanting to keep her little brother safe when she'd not been there for him before."

Sammy watched Cody. He was going to be his cousin now, but he could see where he was going to be a little bit of a pain in the backside. He was forever stealing food out of the house and eating it. He could, he supposed, understand that a little bit.

But all he had to do was ask, and Grandma Morgan would give it to him. Being hungry all the time could make a person stuff themselves, not knowing where their next meal was coming from.

"Hey, stop that." He looked over at Wendy when she yelled at the brownie and decided to check out what was going on with her and Cody. Sammy hated to leave what he was doing, but his sisters might need his protection, and he wasn't going to let them be hurt. She was having an argument with one of the many brownies in the yard today. Cody was just watching the exchange. The brownie reached up and grabbed a handful of his sister's hair and yanked on it. "I told you to stop that. I don't care if you are the favorite of all the brownies. You're not going to steal my hair to make you a rug from it."

"You let her go right now before I go and tell on you." The brownie, Sammy thought his name was Pooh, just glared at Cody. "I said that you're to let her go and get away from here before I swat you. You're not being nice at all."

"I don't care for what you're telling me to

do. Her hair will make a nice rug in my house, and everyone will be so jealous. If she would just let me have some, then she'd not be hurting. This is all her fault." Cody smacked at the little man. After he went flying across the yard, he came back with a small knife in his hand. "You're going to pay for that. I get what I want, and I want this."

Before he could tell the little brownie to stop what he was doing, Cody stepped in front of Wendy and put up his fists. It wasn't going to work, fighting a brownie like this, but Sammy noticed something that no one else had. Tellus, the queen of all, appeared in the yard.

"If you hurt her again, I'm going to tell my Grandma on you. When she finds out what you're doing, she'll be powerful mad at you." Pooh told him he wasn't afraid of anyone. "You'd best be. My grandma is Grandma Morgan, and she's the queen of all the shifters. They just told me that yesterday."

"Like I care." He cut Cody twice more with his blade, and that was when Sammy stepped in. While he was sure that Cody could have handled it, he didn't want to have him hurt. So instead of yelling at him, Sammy told the little man to stop in the most angry voice that he could. "You can't talk to me that way. You're not playing fair. I want what I want, and you're messing things up for me. How am I to get a mate if—"

Sammy had had enough. He used some of his new power on the brownie. "Begone from this land, Pooh. Begone to never return. You have hurt someone that I love for no reason than you could. Begone, and don't you dare come back, or I'll hurt you." The little brownie disappeared, and Cody fell to the ground. "Here, let me look at this for you. I know that it hurts like the dickens but let me make sure that it's not infected or something. That would be just like that thing to hurt you badly."

After getting the wounds cleaned up, Sammy helped his sister up from the ground. While she carried Sara, he let Cody lean on him as they made their way to the house. The cuts were bleeding badly now, and he was as worried as he'd ever been.

~*~

Tellus said nothing as she watched Sammy fuss over Cody and his cuts. The wounds were indeed infected. It looked as if Pooh had tipped his blade in poison from the trees before coming to confront young Wendy. When that didn't work for him, he took on Cody. However, Tellus was most proud of the way that Sammy had handled things.

Cody didn't cry, though she knew that he wanted to. Sammy kept telling him that he had him and that he'd not have to worry about the little brownie again. Then when the faeries showed up to help with the poison, he told the young boy that he didn't need to steal from the house anymore. That he'd show him how to get food that was all around the Leap. Wendy, it seemed, had been cut as well, but there was very little poison in her bloodstream.

"Are you upset with me?" Tellus asked Sammy why he'd think that. Cody was being worked on exclusively by the faerie now. Tellus moved them all into the kitchen of Morgan's home as it was chilly out. Sammy shrugged and thought his words out carefully before he spoke. "I don't know what made me say those words to Pooh, but I have a feeling had he been able to be around the compound much more, he'd really hurt someone. Like a bunch of someones."

"I will tell you something, Sammy, that I don't say all that often to anyone, but I love you, Sammy. And love you even more for what you did for your family today. Not only that, but I was on my way to find out from Morgan what was going on with the faeries that were here working today. Several hundred of them have been ill, and some have even died from what Pooh did to them. He poisoned their waterway for no other reason than he could. However, no one thought to stand up to him like you did. And as you said, he would have gone on hurting people had you not banished him."

"He hurt my sister and cousin." Tellus pulled the young boy up on her lap and held him while the faeries did their work. It would take a great deal of magic for them to make sure that neither one of them died, and when Sammy leapt from her lap to bring out the juice from the refrigerator, she could have turned over her kingdom to him for his quick thinking. "They're going to need this. Wendy and Cody too. Grandma makes the best because it's fresh."

Sammy made his little sister a sippy cup full of juice as well. When he crawled back up into her lap, Tellus held him all the tighter. She told him what the poison was and how it had killed her faeries that had been working. Tellus also made sure that when his parents came into the room, hearing about the commotion, she told them too what fast thinking the two young men, not boys anymore, had done to save Wendy.

"That's terrible." Sammy tired to blow it off as if what he'd done wasn't such a big deal. All the while, he never took his eyes off his little family. When Butter came to sit on her shoulder, she explained for the third time what had happened and that Pooh was no longer a part of the faeries that she loved.

After Cody was put on the couch with Wendy and given a book, Tellus went to talk to the young man. Thad had told her that he didn't think Sammy would take the job from him, and it upset the elderly

gnome a great deal. If today didn't prove that Sammy
was ready to protect all that was her people, she
didn't know what would.

"You thought quickly and saved lives." He
told Tellus that he'd not thought beyond making
sure that his cousin and sister were all right. "That's
what I mean. You didn't think of the consequences
of sending someone away. You saw a need and took
care of it. That is what a good leader would to. I'm so
impressed that you even called for the faeries when
Pooh was gone to make sure that everyone was
all right. Much like you did when Mr. Weeds was
nearly killed by the dogs that day. You think quickly,
Sammy, and I couldn't have been more proud of
you when you didn't ask me to take over when you
saw me. You're a good man. A better leader than I
thought you to be. You must take the job that Thad
is offering you. I know that I will rest better knowing
that you won't second guess yourself but take it upon
yourself to get the job done. Good job on that. I have
a reward for you."

"No." She nearly laughed when he got off her

lap and put his hands behind his back. Remembering what had happened the last time she rewarded him, his eyes held a tiny bit of fear. "I got enough rewards, thanks. If you want to reward someone, then give it to Cody. He was there and trying to help Wendy. I only came in when he was being hurt."

"Then you reward him. For valor." He asked her what that meant. "It's for courage in the face of danger. Both of you did that today. Came to the rescues of not just family but for all. I might not have figured out who had harmed the faeries if I had not heard you yelling for help. If you'd not sent him away when you did, it's difficult to know how long it would have taken me to figure out who the culprit had been. As you have pointed out, he could have gone on killing, and it might well have been too late for many of the creatures that work and play here."

"Do you know why he wanted Wendy's hair?" She said that he did want it for his rug but not until she was dead. "He couldn't kill her."

"No. But he could have hurt her badly in the process of trying to end her life. As it was now, he's gone, and we don't have to worry about him any longer. I, for one, am happy for the outcome of today."

The rest of the day was spent with the children playing out in the light snow. Tellus knew that Sammy was keeping an eye on his sisters and cousin. He was never more than a few feet from them at any given time. And to watch him playing with Cody had Tellus thinking that even though they started out on the wrong foot, with the two of them clashing, she'd bet that they'd be lifelong friends now.

"I've been meaning to ask you. I know that I should have before now, but when a creature is banished, what happens to them?" Morgan had come out on the deck where a fire had been lit in a pit, handing her not just a cup of tea but some of her famous cookies as well. "I don't know that I've ever banished anyone with the thought of where they end up. And while we're on the subject, can you banish humans?"

"They are dead." Morgan nearly dropped her tea cup when Tellus told her. "There is nowhere on this earth that someone or something can go that wouldn't make them still a part of my world. There would be nowhere else to send them to for that very reason." Tellus hurt to talk about it, but Morgan did need to know. "They just disappear from the earth, much like humans do. However, there is no one to mourn their passing nor a grave where they might be lying to rest. Once they have been banished, their home, possessions, as well as anything that they might have created, disappears with them. Not mates or children, of course. Unless, of course, they are a part of whatever the person was doing. But overall, they just are no more."

"While I understand that, it's still frightening to know the information as well." Tellus looked at Morgan, a woman who had become her best friend over the years. She had...well, she'd not known what to expect. This woman of the earth was forever surprising her. "I'm glad that I asked. I'll make sure I think about that if it ever comes up again. I don't know that I could do it with what I have in the way of powers, but I will consider it better when I hear it being done. I don't think that anyone should tell Sammy. He might not take it so well."

"No, I'm not going to do that. I don't want you to do it either, not even to hint at it, Morgan." She asked her why not as she sat her cup down on the table, her anger at this idea in her stance and face. "Because do you think that he would have been able to save those children had he had to think about whether or not it was worth the brownie dying for? It might well have been too late for one or both of those children. My faeries are alive, hundreds of them, I'm thinking, because Sammy knew what had to be done, and he did it. His wording was correct. On point to the situation. I doubt very much, if given the circumstance to someone else, say one of your sons, they would have done it so quickly. Not because they didn't want to end the world of this monster's terror, but they would have thought of the pain it would have caused someone to know that their child, friend, or lover was going to die."

"Are you saying that Sammy is cold-hearted?" Tellus stood as well, her anger right there in the forefront. "I'm sorry. I'm rattled today. Starting out a day having to save one of my own scared me to overthinking things. Do forgive me, Tellus. I'm so very sorry I said that."

"Thank you for that, Morgan. But I do not think that he is cold-hearted at all. I think that he has a man's mind and will act accordingly to the situation. Thaddeus trained him well. I think, too, that you have had a heavy hand in his training as well. I see you out there talking to him and the earth. You're doing so well with a child of your heart. I cannot imagine how you...what am I thinking. There would have been no difference between a child of your heart or one of your son's body. I beg your forgiveness in thinking that. Even for a moment, my friend. They are all your grandchildren, no matter how they came to you."

"They are. I will admit that I'm enjoying the little girls a tad more than the boys at the moment. I've never been around little girls before. All I've had around me for centuries are boys and men. Well, you, but you've always been an adult, I think." They both laughed. "I've been putting pretty things, little dresses and the like in my to-make pile. I have ordered myself some beautiful material so that I can make them things." Tellus envied Morgan in that moment. She'd never been one to be jealous of anything or anyone, and here she was for the first time —

"What's this?" Bethy had just started walking a few days ago, she knew. Today, she had toddled her way to her, falling only once, but she got up and waddled her way to her. Tellus picked up the tiny little human and held her up so they could look into each other's eyes. "For one so young, my child, you have the eyes of a person who has seen war, and it hurts you still."

Bethy touched her finger to her check, taking the small tear there to her mouth and licking it clean. The wave of magic and energy, too, rolled over them both, and Tellus was glad that she had been holding onto her, or there was no telling what might have happened to the baby. Sitting her in the rocking chair next to her, Tellus stared at the child. Morgan asked her what was wrong.

"Nothing. I had it in my head to take away the horror of her life thus far, but I think that would be a mistake. It will form her, I've no doubt, into a woman that will go far with whatever she decides to do. Her mate, too, he'll see her strength like none other will." Kissing the child on the forehead, Tellus stood up with a smile on her face. "Aye, she'll be a good mother, wife, friend, as well as granddaughter to you, Morgan, queen of the shifters."

After leaving the compound, Tellus made her way to her own garden. There she had plants that were no longer in the world beyond her. Someday, she might well give them over to them once again, but she'd wait until Bethy was old enough to find them. The child, as she had told Morgan, would be a good person, better than most. Tellus decided that she'd teach her the plants and their line of linage. It never hurts to have someone knowing that sort of information in both worlds, she thought. She was going to start on her education as soon as tomorrow.

Chapter 2

Marley was making his way to the hospital when he noticed a home was being built. He'd had the occasion to see one go up before and had even built a few of the buildings around here in his youth. But the house in front of him was being built without magic. Just a normal everyday home being put together by men.

"You thinking what I'm thinking?" He glanced at his brother Carroll and told him he doubted anyone thought on his lines of thinking. "Very funny. I was just thinking about Mom and Tom. Last night when I came in to go to bed, they were on the couch, sitting very close and talking. I don't think they were doing anything more than that, but Tom and Mom both jumped up from it like they'd been lit on fire. I was embarrassed, and I'm sure they were as well."

"What does that have to do with me watching a house go up?" Carroll hesitated for a few moments, and he saw one of the men on the ground level cry out in pain. Making his way to the man to see what was going on, he felt his brother right behind him.

After sending the man to the emergency room, he started walking in that direction as well. Carroll never left his side. He asked him again what he was talking about with the house.

"I'm going to build myself and Hanna a home. Of our own." That had Marley stopping to look at his older brother. "There is no way for us to get to our rooms except through the living room. Where they were, I'm going to point that out again. I suppose we could magically make us an entrance, but I was thinking that now that we're starting to get our mates, we need to get out of mom's home and have one of our own. I was thinking of other things that might be advantageous to having our own space. One of them is giving mom and Tom some privacy. However, I'm not talking like building far away. She'll be able to come to see us anytime she wants."

"She can do that now." Carroll smiled but didn't say anything more. "Have you talked to her about this? Telling her a reason why you want to have your own home? Because if you tell her that you want to give her some privacy, I think she'll never be close to Tom again for fear that one or all of us will leave her. She's been upset by that thought before."

"I know. That's why I came to you about it." Marley said that he wasn't going to talk to her about it either. "I didn't think you would. No, I was thinking that the women should. They're better at being straight up than we are. I'd be fumbling all over myself, trying to find the way to say it without her being hurt. I know she will, and that is the only reason that I've not done it myself."

Veni and Zippy both were standing at the

entrance to the hospital when they got there. Neither of them looked all that happy. As Marley was going over everything that he'd said to anyone over the last day or two, Veni kissed him on the cheek.

"You worry too much." He told Veni that she could kill him. "I'd not do that. Not unless it was necessary. It's not necessary, is it, little brother?"

"No. And stop scaring me. It's hard enough to go to work every day knowing that I have a mate at home without you making me think of ways that you could hurt me. Why are you even here today? I have a full workload." Veni told him that they were going to have lunch with Morgan today and talk about housing. Marley looked at his brother. "He didn't tell me. Hanna did. She said that Carroll talks to himself, and she put it together from what he was saying. Would you like a home of your own?"

"Are you going to be coming by all the time to check on us? Make sure that we're doing what is right?" She asked him why she'd do that. "I don't know, Veni. You're a scary grand witch, and I'm nothing more than a leopard that is terrified of you."

When she kissed him on the cheek and walked away, he was more afraid of her than he'd been before. Simply because she'd not answered his question. Going into the emergency room, he was ready to turn around and leave again when he saw that the place was packed with people sitting in wheelchairs. He was grabbed by the ear by Nurse Duncan.

She was terrifying too. Just being only a human, he'd seen her make grown men piss themselves with just a look. One time, he nearly got shot by one of the people he'd been working on, and all she did was walk up behind the man, chop him in the neck like he'd seen on a couple of science fiction shows, and he dropped like a dead log. Handing him the gun, she told him he'd best be keeping it because she might not be around the next time he needed her. She was legendary when it came to new nurses on staff too.

Dolores would take them under her wing when they joined the team. Showing them the ropes, picking up after them and so on. But once you cross a line, whatever line you had to cross with her, she was finished with your ass. And the nurse would be gone before the next payroll came around. Dolores did not suffer fools or liars well.

"Doctor Golden, you're leaving that pretty mate at home all on her own today?" Marley told her that she was packing up her business back at her home. "Good girl, that one. She's going to give you pretty babies, I think too. Your momma, she sure does love them grandbabies of hers. My kids ain't got the gumption of two sloths to make me any grandbabies. I swear to you, Doctor Golden, they're going to make me die, not being able to hold me just one of them like your momma does. I just know it."

"You come on over to the house sometime. I'll make sure that she shares one or two with you when you get there. She'll do it for you, I think, because she loves you. Not so much for others around town." She was still laughing as he made his way to the nurse's breakroom to get the rundown on the day. The nurse in charge of the floor was telling them about an accident up on Route Forty, and they could be getting people in most of the morning. Not being an emergency room doctor, he asked her where she wanted him. "I'm willing to be just about anyplace you need me if you give me a nurse that knows where to find things when I need them. I haven't spent a lot of time in this area."

For the next ten hours, he went from cubical to cubical. Marley was the triage doctor. He would decide who was going to be seen first by the medical team or who might need surgery right away. Even worse, he was there to be with someone when they were taking their last breath. A job that he hated more than anything else.

When things started to slow down, Marley made his way to the cafeteria. It was the kind of place where they cooked the meals there instead of having them shipped in from a larger facility. Today's special, he noticed, was a cold meatloaf sandwich served on freshly baked bread with bread and butter pickles, mashed potatoes, green beans and a drink. Ordering two whole meals, he was a big eater being a cat, he was just sitting down to enjoy his meal when Sin sat across from him.

"I swear to Christ, there are days when I want

to murder someone." She asked him if he was going to eat both potatoes, and he handed her one of the plates to take both of his. "These are really good. I decided that I can't have a mover pack up my things to bring here. One company sent three men over, and they were fucking drunk. The second company decided that they'll do the packing for me, but they're going to charge me per pound. Who does that kind of shit? These are really good potatoes, Marley. Not as good as your moms are, but really close."

"The potatoes, beef and green beans come from our place. The butter, too, I think. We don't do pickles, mom can't stand the smell of them, but they're not bad. Who did you end up with in getting you packed up?" She told him between bites. After she took one of his sandwiches, he didn't wait for her to answer anything else but went to the counter to get two more meals. "All right. So you had the faeries pack you up and bring it back here. I don't want to say I told you so, but I did suggest that before you left. Are you going to eat all that?"

Smiling at him, she handed him back one of

the sandwiches that were on the plate. After he had eaten his first one, then the second one, he decided to wait to see how much she ate of the third one before he took it. He could always get himself some snacks on the floor but watching her enjoy his meal was kind of sexy.

"They did such a wonderful job that I'm going to use them for my house too. I swear to you, Marley, if I had to eat here daily, I'd weigh a ton in no time." He told her that she'd never gain any weight unless she was carrying a child. "Great. That means I can have a piece of the lemon pie that I can see from here. That's another thing I want to talk to you about. Why aren't we having copious amounts of sex? I guess the others are having it several times a day. Do you not think I'm sexy enough for you?"

Her pouting lower lip tempted him. But it was the glaze from the sandwich on her lips that had him groaning about how sexy she looked to him. Standing up, leaning over the table toward her, he first licked the red sauce off her mouth and then devoured her mouth. Sitting down, his cock was hard as stone right now and was aching badly enough that he was sure that he was going to come at any moment. She just stared at him. Her mouth slack, and the sandwich she'd been eating hanging off her fingers.

"Does that answer your question, love?" She nodded, the sandwich forgotten. "Eat your dinner, Sin, before I take you right here on this table. I'm not ignoring you. I think you're beautiful and sexy, but I won't jump you unless you want it. Since we've both been getting our life straightened out, I've not been able to be around you nearly as much as I'd like."

She was still sitting there when his name was announced over the public address system. Heading to the emergency room, Marley kept thinking about the look on Sin's face when he kissed her. He'd been wanting to do that for weeks now, and getting to do it while at work wouldn't be good for the rest of his night. Working twelves was hard on a body, but he also knew that he'd have the next three days off in a row to take up where he'd left off with the kiss.

He'd been called away to do a pronouncement. The patient had been killed while jogging and hadn't been wearing any kind of reflective gear. It was a hit and run, but the part where they were going to find the driver was out of his hands. Going into the next cubical, he saw his brother there with Hanna. She'd fallen off the deck, and they were making sure that the baby was all right before Carroll had a massive stroke with his worrying.

"I told him that I can feel the baby is all right. I can do that now. But he insisted. Aren't we all immortal?" While he was setting up the ultrasound to see the baby, he told her that the child was not immortal until it took its first breath. "Oh. I don't think I knew that. I'll be more careful from now — is that his heart beating?"

It was. It was a strong heartbeat that had all three of them laughing. When he moved, Marley paused for a moment to have a look around. That was when he saw baby number two and number three. Wondering how he was going to tell them that they were having triplets, he saw baby number four. Looking at his brother, he had to laugh.

"Don't freak out on me." Carroll said he wasn't

in the habit of freaking out. "No, but you were freaked out when Hanna fell. Just take a deep breath, and I'll tell you what I've found. All right?"

"Just tell me, not him." He said that he couldn't do that. Not with this. "Is the baby all right? The doctor said that I was large for my due date and that they'll be taking another ultrasound soon. What is it, Marley? I'm freaking out."

"You're having quadruplets. Four that I've found so far." Carroll laughed and told him he wasn't funny. "I'm being serious. I've found four heartbeats, and while all of them are strong and healthy sounding, you're going to have to take it easy from now on. You're only going to get bigger and clumsier, and you'll need to take better care of yourself. Not that you don't now, but this is going to be a great deal of drain on you, and I don't want you harmed nor the babies."

"Four. You're sure? What am I saying? Of course, you're sure." He showed them both the heartbeats of all four children. It was easy for him to see that there were four different heartbeats because he'd done this before. But to them, Carroll said he thought that the baby was moving around."

All he did was say Veni's name, and she appeared in the room with them. Telling her what he'd found, she smiled at Carroll and Hanna and said that she'd known it for a while now. There were four babies, two girls and two boys and that they were healthy as shit. He wasn't entirely sure what that meant, but she did put her hands on Hanna's belly and let her feel what she knew.

"They're too small for me to tell you in what order they'll be born, but I'll be able to tell in a few months." Marley left the couple alone when Veni left. She did tell them that Hanna would need to rest a good deal more than she was. Also, she'd need to eat more red meat. The beef that came from the leap was better for her and the babies because it wasn't like some stores sell, full of chemicals. He was forever happy that his family made sure that not just the world around them was better but the people that lived there as well.

~*~

Piper did love the way she was looking with this forced diet that she was on, but she'd never tell anyone that. Not only was she losing weight, but she felt better than she had in a very long time. More like forever, she thought. But she wasn't going to just roll over and be fucked from behind, either. There were things going on that she didn't care for. One of them was people telling her that her children were better off without her. Then there was her mom.

Mom had been away from her since the start of this nightmare. Not once had she been able to talk to her nor just to see her. Piper wanted to show off her new body and tell her mom that the kids were coming home with her when she got out of here. She was even going to convince her mom that she needed to take the rap for all this so that she could raise her babies.

Piper didn't want to be a mom, but while in jail, she'd heard that she'd be entitled to a food card, a nice house, and all her bills paid off, like cable and shit like that. She'd just hire some kid to watch them when she wanted to party. Surely they'd pay for that too.

It didn't bother her about the welfare department taking away her mom's card from before. She was a mom now, and they had to take care of her like she needed to be taken care of. The thing that she was looking forward to the most was the house. She'd seen pictures of them after looking them up on the internet. They only had an hour a day to be on one, and she liked looking at the things that she was going to be getting for free. Piper would have to ask next time they were all together if they would give her a nice car too. That would be the perfect ending for this shit going on around here.

When she'd been younger, about ten, she supposed, she and her mom had an okay house that the government paid for. It didn't cost them anything monthly, but they had none of the other treats that she was looking forward to getting. Whatever the food amount was on this card, she was going to eat what she wanted but in moderation.

Standing up when she was told, something that she'd learned the hard way, was to do what they told you. She was told to go back to the back wall. She hated to do that, it made her stand next to her toilet, and it smelled. She'd never had to clean up after herself before and hadn't the first clue how she was supposed to clean the sucker.

She was handed a pair of new pants as well as a pretty blouse. When it wouldn't fit, she ended up having to wear her orange and blue jumpsuit. Christ, that thing made her look like a fool. But since the pants were too small and the blouse was way too big, she had to make do. The ride over to the courthouse was made in silence. Not that she didn't want to talk to someone other than other inmates, but they wouldn't answer her questions, so Piper didn't bother.

The courthouse was packed today. As it had been yesterday when her court hearing had been cancelled because things had run over. She wanted to talk about that too. Since she was the one that had to wait on them to get their shit together while she sat in jail, they should be at least nice enough to let her have a night out on the town before going back to her stupid cell. When she heard her name called practically before she was even seated, Piper used that time to make sure that the judge knew what sort of things she wanted to do when they finally let her out.

"I'm sorry. Whatever gave you the idea that you were going to be set free? Certainly wasn't me, as this is the first time that I've spoken to you." She said she had babies to care for and that she wanted to get herself one of those food cards so that she could eat. Then she amended it to say to feed her babies. "The adorable little girls that have been adopted? The children that you quite quickly turned over to Morgan and her family? Those children? They've been adopted by the family and are no longer yours to be concerned with."

"I want them back. I mean, please, I'd like to get them back so that I can raise them on my own. I get a food card and a house if I have them back with me. I'm going to talk to my mom about taking the rap for the shit that we did when we was free. She'll do that because I'm her only child."

"You think that your mom will just say, 'Hey, yes, anything for you. I'd gladly add whatever years you were going to serve on top of my already outlandish amount of time. You go on ahead and be a good mom.'" Piper said that was exactly what her mom would say. "I doubt it, but let's see together, why don't we. Bring Ms. Mission in, please."

Her mom looked terrible. Not only had her hair turned nearly all white, but it was sticking up all over the place like she'd only just rolled out of bed. Piper had at least taken the time to comb her hair and pull it back. What she wouldn't do for a nice hair cut and her nails done. But her mother looked like she was as old as grandma did when she passed. They looked at one another, and it took her mom a few moments to realize who she was.

"My god, Piper, you looked like jail time has agreed with you. How much weight have you lost?" She told her mom that it was about a hundred pounds. But she wasn't eating like she wanted to. "You should lay off the sweets. I've always told you that. But to look at you now, I'm betting that it's too bad that you're going to prison. You could get that man now for sure."

"That's what I want to talk to you about, Mom." She looked up at the judge, who was eyeing them both like she was watching a tennis match. Piper thought she was enjoying this too much with her chin perched on her hand. "Can I have a few minutes alone?"

"No. You're not going to have a few minutes alone with anyone, Piper. Just talk to your mom so that we can move on with this hearing today." She looked at her mom. "Hurry it along. I've got a full docket today."

"Mom, I've decided to get my kids back." Mom told her that she couldn't think she could raise them in prison. "No. No, that's not what I was thinking. What I was thinking is that you'd take the amount that I'm supposed to be guilty for and add them to your years or whatever you get. You want me to be out and about, don't you? Meeting new people? Being happy to be free? I mean, you can't want your only child to be in prison with you when I can be out in the world making a life for myself? Would you?"

"You mean with your kids?" Piper asked her mom what she meant. "You said that you wanted your kids back. I'm assuming that you must have a plan for them while you're out and about. Meeting people and making friends. What about those children that you never wanted? What happens to them?"

"Oh, they'll be all right. I mean, I'll find a good sitter when I go out. But think about it. I'll have a nice house to live in. A food card. I even heard that they sometimes give you money so that you can have little treats for yourself." Mom looked at the judge, and so did she. The woman was still staring at them like she was enjoying herself too much. "I'll be able to have all that and more if I were to be free of prison. Right?"

"Let us clear up one thing at a time, why don't we?" The judge looked at mom again. "Ms. Mission, are you willing, if it's something that I agree to, to take on your daughter's prison time as your own if I were to okay that? I'm not saying that I will. There are a great many things to consider in these two cases, but would you do that? Before you answer, your daughter seems to think that you're going to take hers fifty years to life on just because she asked you to?"

Mom just looked at her. But before she could explain more what her plans were, remembering at the last minute that she should have told her that she'd come to visit her with the brats — babies when she could get around to it, her mother slapped her across the face. She asked her what that was for.

"You honestly think that you'd be a good mother to those little girls? I don't. I think that the first time you had to change a shitty diaper, you'd be selling them off like we planned to do before my mom called about the Morgan family." Piper didn't think this was the time to bring it up but told her that she'd have someone else to do those sorts of things. "You're going to have yourself a Nanny too? Good Christ, Piper, why didn't I think of that. Be on welfare because there isn't any money coming in and hiring a nanny. I'm supposing you'll want a maid too? Someone to clean up after you and the brats. A person to cook for you. Because I know for a fact that you've not the first clue on how to make something to eat. You do realize, too, that those brats will need clothing as well. Baths once or more a day. They can't eat food until they're like six months old, so that'll have to be fed to them. Also, you might not have thought about this, but there is formula and shit—"

"I'm going to get a food card. There will be plenty of money on that for everything they need. If not, I'll go down to the office and tell them it's not cutting it. I've seen people do that before." Mom told her that she wouldn't be able to get money to pay for diapers or clothing. How was that going to work? "You're being very negative about everything I want to do. I might have to get a job working a couple of hours a week. That's all."

"Is this job going to be paying you about a grand an hour? Because otherwise, Piper, that's not going to be nearly enough to raise a baby, much less two of them. Clothes are expensive. Not to mention car seats, baby beds and all the other crap they'll need. I think a bag of diapers is about twenty bucks nowadays." The judge told her mom they were forty dollars for a little over a hundred diapers. But that would only last for about a week or so. "A week for forty bucks. That's for just one, I'm assuming." The judge nodded.

"I'll figure it out. That's not what I'm asking you. And thank you so much for raining on my parade, Mom. I thought of all people you'd be the most supportive. Are you going to help me out or not?" She said that she wouldn't. Then she laughed. "Why not? And why do you find this so funny? I'm trying to get my life back together. Don't you understand?"

"What I understand is that you're not thinking beyond the fact that you think you're going to be entitled to all this. You aren't. We have, the two of us have been banded from getting any kind of government support because we abused the system. Hasn't your attorney told you that? Mine did. He said that if I were ever to entertain the thought of getting out of prison in a single lifetime, I'd not be put into any kind of government housing. I'd get no assistance. As soon as I got out, if I was upright, I'd be on my own. You too, he told me."

"Well, that's not fair. Christ, how the hell will I be able to afford shit after all this?" The judge said she'd not have to worry about that. "Why? Do you know of some way that I'm going to be able to have a life of my own? That I can go out and party and shit?"

"No. As I said before, I don't know how you figured you were ever getting out of prison to have anything resembling a life. Between the two of you, there are nine dead people that have families that need to have closure. Someone needs to pay for the crimes committed against them. And lucky for us, you two are the ones that are going to do it. Since you both have agreed not to have a trial, Meredith Mission, you are hereby sentenced to ninety-nine life sentences or six thousand ninety years in prison. There will be no parole hearing for you because that is going to be denied to you as well. Your term will start the moment you leave this courtroom." She looked at her, and Piper was trying to think how she'd come up with that many years. Then it hit her. Ninety-nine life sentences were seventy years for each sentence. Christ, her mother was never getting out.

"Are you listening to me, Piper Mission?" She said that she wasn't, but she would now. "Good. You are here by sentenced to sixty life sentences or forty-two hundred years. You are also denied parole—"

"That's not right. That means I'm never getting out. I mean, I can see it for my mom. She's old anyway, but I can't serve forty-two hundred years. That's not even possible." She said that she knew that. "Then why don't you just say until you die or something like that? It's not right that you tack on that many years like there is anyone alive to make it that far."

"Does is scare you to know that you're going to be spending that much time in prison? That you have no chance of getting out no matter how many years you might live? I hope it does. Because it makes me sleep better at night knowing that people like you and your mother will be behind bars long after I'm dust. Years and years after the people that I know will be gone. Yes, I love being able to sentence you to that many years." She laughed. "If you think about it, it gives you something to look forward to, maybe. You can start marking little lines on your cell walls. You can tell yourself that you have only three thousand nine hundred and ninety-nine years to go, and so on. Yes, it makes me feel very good to give you and your mother a long sentence."

Piper found herself on the bus on her way to someplace before she could ask any questions. Not that her mind would slow enough for her to think of them right now. But all she could think about was that this had to be some kind of joke. How the hell was she going to party and have a life if she was in prison for so long. She needed answers and was going to get them. As soon as she figured out what the fuck was going on.

Chapter 3

Marley was nervous. It wasn't as if he'd not thought of making love to Sin since he'd met her, but things had kept getting in the way. Mostly it was things that they had no control over, but there were things that he knew weren't anything but nerves keeping them apart. When Danish asked him if he needed anything from him, he smiled.

"I'd like for you to make sure that our home is cleaned up. After that, I'd like for you to make sure that there are things that we can eat without too much trouble in the master bedroom." Danish blushed but nodded. "Neither of us drinks, so I'd like for there to be water chilled as well as roses all over the bedroom. In moderation, Danish. I don't want to have to move through a forest to get to the bed."

"Yes, I can do that. As well as some chocolates for the two of you. I have noticed that Lady Sin enjoys a bit of it after dinner. The darkest is the best, she told Donut once." He'd not known that, so he was glad for the information. "Also, my lord, there are some of the faeries that are wondering about the land that you have set aside for your home. I have been informed that you wish to talk to your mother first."

"Yes. I hadn't any idea that there was anything earmarked for me, but that's good to know. I have to talk to mom soon. Don't do anything until after I have a word with her. She might not understand what is going on, and I don't want her upset." He heard the front door open and Sin call out for him. After telling her where he was, she came into the living room and sat on his lap, facing him. Danish disappeared.

"I've gotten nothing done today, just thinking about jumping your bones." Marley told her that he loved the way her mind worked. He pulled her closer to him and kissed her with all the passion that he'd been storing up for her. "Yes, I needed that too. But that's not enough. I need you. Now."

Instead of going up to their bedroom, which more than likely was finished, he lifted up her blouse, cupping her breast so that they were still hidden from him, but he could see their fullness. Licking them, tasting of her flesh, he felt his cock engorge to the point of pain. Christ, he wanted this woman more than he thought he did his next breath.

"You need to have me." When Sin unhooked her bra from behind, he still played with the tops of her breasts. They were full and firm, and he couldn't wait to suckle the tips of them. As he moved her blouse and bra up, her moaning was nearly his undoing. "Please, you can play around later. I am so needy right now, Marley, that I think that waiting much longer will kill me."

Still, he played. Having her so ready to come

was enjoyable for him. He'd been in a state of ready to do just that for the last several days. He thought he might hold the record for taking cold showers of anyone in the world. Lying her on the couch as her blouse moved up and over her head, he rolled around until he was between her legs.

Sin's breasts were pink. Her nipples were hard and long. The thought of taking one into his mouth was almost too much for him to ignore. But he waited to give himself that pleasure. There was more of her to taste and to make love to than her beautiful breasts, and he was going to explore every inch of her.

Taking off her pants and panties, he could only stare at the way she looked. Naked and wet, all he could think about was that she was his. That forever, it would be just her in his life and any children that she wanted to have with him. Kissing her navel, as close as he wanted to get to her breasts, he made his way to her hipbone as he told her what he was going to do to her.

"First, I'm going to feast on you. I'm going to drink down every one of your climaxes until you're too weak to move. After that, I'm going to taste your thighs, your knees, the back of your knees to your feet. I cannot wait to get to your pretty feet and fuck them with my cock." She moaned, making him ache all the more. "After that, I'm going to make my way up your body to those lovely breasts. I might spend all day on them. After, if it ever comes to pass, I have my fill of them, I'm going to slide my thick cock into you and feel you come all over my cock. Would you like that, baby?"

"Please. Now." He kissed her navel again. Once he had her squirming around, he slid his tongue over her hip to her pussy. Marley could smell her then. Her scent was too much and not enough at the same time. Lifting her up just enough where he could lick her from gate to clit, he lingered over her hard nubbin until she screamed out his name. Marley took her into his mouth and suckled hard on her pussy.

Sin came so many times that he was near drunk on her juices. Each time he touched her with his tongue or finger, she came screaming. Each time she would beg him to stop, only to start begging him to give her more. Since he was in control right now, he did what he wanted, and that was to eat her until she was limp with it. The hand to his hair being yanked up, he looked at her.

Her eyes were glazed over. Her lower lip had just a drop of blood on it. He wanted to taste that, too but didn't want to leave where he was at the moment. When she spoke, he had to ask her to repeat herself. His body was in overload, and he wasn't sure he'd heard her right.

"Fuck me, I said. Or I'm going to hurt you." He grinned at her. "You're not all that charming, buddy. Get to fucking me, or I'll find someone that will."

Giving her pussy one more swipe of his tongue, he made his way up her body. Pausing at her hipbone again, he laved his tongue over it several times before moving to her navel. He didn't spend as much time as he wanted there but made his way to her breasts. That was where his goal had been.

Cupping them both in his hands, he alternated between the right and then the left one. Suckling at them hard enough that she would pull him away.

Her feet on his cock had him remembering his plan, but they were both too far gone for him to make his way back down her body. Even as he suckled at her nipples, he moved his body so that his cock was at her entrance.

The heat was more than he could have anticipated. She was wet too. Moving slowly, just the head of his cock in and out of her, Sin wrapped her legs around him and pushed upwards. Marley felt his eyes roll to the back of his head and stay there. He was unable to move, even to take in a breath was too much for him. Instead of trying to take her again, he kissed her with all the passion he felt since he'd touched her flesh.

"Please?" It was all she had to say for him to take her. Filling her over and over again was more than he could have thought of making love. She clung to him as he took her. Her hands and mouth moved over parts of his body that she could reach until he was ready to beg her to stop. Then, before he could do anything, his body paused long enough for his breath to catch, his body to stiffen. Marley let go of his body into hers until he was positive that he was going to be sore in the morning. Still, he didn't stop.

Her body was hard too. The need that she had was almost something that he could touch and taste. Even as he lifted up her bottom to fill her tightly, he knew that she was as close to the edge as he was again. Marley wanted to come with her. To hit their peak at the same time. And when Sin threw back her head, her body nearly bent in half, he watched with fascination as she not only came hard but she dug her nails deeply into his shoulders until he came with her. Christ, he wasn't sure that he was ever going to stop. His poor abused body simply shut down atop her.

Waking up, he didn't move. It wasn't that he couldn't, but he wasn't sure that he wanted to risk it. Even his toes, when he curled them to stretch out his feet, seemed to scream in protest. Lying still, he used his eyes, painful too, to find where he was and where his lovely mate was.

Moving his fingers when he wasn't able to see

her, she told him not to touch her. Ever again. The laughter made his ribs hurt like he'd been beaten near to death, but he asked her if she was all right.

"No. You must have broken me. I've been contemplating getting up to pee for the last ten minutes, but it hurts too much." She moaned again, this time in obvious pain. "What did you do to me? I feel relaxed and in pain at the same time. Also, I don't know about you, but I think you broke me. I'm not going to be able to have sex again."

"You'll be fine in an hour or two." She told him she needed to pee now. "I can't help you there, honey. I'm about to bust myself." Giggling, he finally made himself sit up. But not without a great deal of pain. "I had no idea that sex could be that painful, did you?"

"I hate you." She rolled over when he helped her to get to the side of the bed, but he could see tears in her eyes. He told her he was sorry. "No, don't be. I didn't mean to tell you that I hate you. I love you with all my soul. I'm sorry. But I am feeling better now that I'm moving around."

While she made her way, limping to the bathroom, he got up and put the bed to rights. It was still dark out, and he wondered how they'd gotten to their bed. Then he vaguely remembered picking her up and brining her in here about one in the morning. It was five now, so they'd not had a great deal of sleep.

Making the two of them up a tray of little sandwiches, fruit and cheeses, he had it laid out on the bed when she returned. Wearing the shirt he'd had on yesterday, he told her how wonderful she looked.

"You'd not say that if you were to see all the bruises that I have everywhere." He said that he wasn't in much better shape. "I thought you might not be. I was going to take a hot bath, but you don't have a tub. Not that I think that I could get in and out of the sucker, but it was a thought of mine." She winced as she sat down on the bed before continuing. "If we build, I'm not saying that I care one way or the other, but if we do, I want a hot tub right outside our room. That way, I can work out my kinks without letting anyone know I feel abused."

"I'm going to talk to mom soon about us moving out. I haven't any idea how she's going take it, but I hope she doesn't cry. That'll do me in." They finished off most of the cheese and crackers and all the sandwiches. He got up once to get them more to drink and filled the plate up again. By the time they were setting it aside, they were exhausted again and laid back on the bed. "I have two meetings tomorrow with the city. Also, I'm going to talk to my brothers about how they want to handle the witch Connie. I know that she's been out there causing trouble, but as a family, we're going to help Zippy and Veni get their magic ready for her. I don't think it'll take much, not from what I've heard, but I don't want them to get hurt either."

"I don't want them hurt either. I have the last shipment coming in tomorrow from my shop. Also, I'm going to work with the things that have already been brought here. I don't have a lot of orders right now, but I will in a couple of weeks. I've finished with the Spring catalog, so I need to get a head start on Summer and fall. They'll be huge this coming year."

"It's sort of like here, we have to be at least two seasons ahead of things, or there will be no planting." She said that was her way of doing things too. "Is the building going to be large enough for you? I know that the faeries have been excited for you to go over it with them."

"It's larger than I thought it would be, but I can use the extra space. I'm not going to be able to use any of my past employees for her, so I need to get with one of your sisters and have them help me find workers. I won't need that many, to begin with, but in the end, I'll need about fifty. Also, I'm going to hire some of the kids from the high school as models for the catalog. That way, they can get a start on a career if they want and make some money at the same time."

After she yawned a few times, he watched her. He didn't need to sleep, not any of them did, but he did need down time. Having fallen asleep after making love to her was a surprise, but he had worn himself out.

After lying there for about half an hour, he got up. Showering, he went to the kitchen to find a note from Cody. He had stayed the night with Grandma Morgan as Grandpa Tom was out of town to sell his home. Cody, Sin's little brother, was enjoying his time with them, and he hoped that his mother, Melody Bander, would leave him alone to be with them. She didn't seem to want him anyway. But stranger things had happened with people here lately.

After having some breakfast, he made his way down to his mom's part of the house. She and Cody had gone to the orchard and would be back around noon. Good. He had plenty of time to get his shit together before talking to her. And to let the others know that they were going to be there too when they discussed the houses. He only hoped that his mom took it as well as they all hoped.

~*~

Morgan wanted to run from the house every time she was left alone with Tom. Not that she didn't like him, Morgan thought she might be in love for the first time in her life. But he was different than having the boys around her. He was…well, she loved him and wanted more from him than she did anyone in her life up until now. But she wasn't sure how to go about that. Any kind of affection for a man other than her boys was something that she'd never experienced before.

"I must be insane." Marley asked her what she was insane about as he entered the kitchen with her. Tom had gone out to talk to his daughter about some furniture that she was looking at, and Cody went to pester his sister. Morgan thought that was funny. Looking at her son, she remembered that he'd asked her something. "I was just thinking that I need to make more jelly for the winter months. Also that I needed to bake more cookies."

"All right, Mom. How about we break down what you just said to me. First of all, you always have more than enough jelly and jams to go around in the winter months. You even manage to have enough to donate to the local homes when they need it. Number two, I don't know if you realize this or not, but you have enough cookies boxed up now that you could have a store to open up right now and not have to bake for at least the first year." He sat down at her baking table, picked up several of the cookies she'd just finished decorating and produced them both a cup of tea. "I don't know why you think that you need to fib to me about how much you're not enjoying having a man around all the time. I mean, other than us six. The man nearly worships the ground you walk on. But then, he doesn't know you as well as we do. Tell me what's going on. You can trust me not to tell the others. This has seriously upset you."

He patted the chair next to her, and she sat down. Biting the cookie that he handed her as she tried to get her words lined up to speak to him about things. Marley had always been the one person that she could go to and trust when she was upset. Even if it was about him, he would listen to her, let her work things out by talking to him then he'd go about his business. And as he said, he'd not told a single person what they'd talked about.

"It's about Tom, as you've guessed." Marley didn't say anything as he sipped his tea. "I'm in love with him, but I'm not really sure what to do with him."

He laughed. Not just a small one, either. It got to the point in his laughter that she had to bang him on his back to make sure that the cookie that he seemed to inhale didn't strangle him too badly. When he was breathing better, Morgan got up and went to the sink, telling him to get his ass out of the house.

"Mom." He laughed a little more, then straightened up when he looked at her. "Mom. You're going to have to tell me what you mean by you don't know what to do with him.

"It's about Tom. He's been staying here for a few weeks now, but he's been out in the morning before I can talk to him. Then he's off to bed before I am most nights." Marley said that he had seen him about and that he enjoyed the man's company. "I do too. A great deal. I guess everyone knows that he's my mate."

"We do. But it doesn't explain why you're all tensed up all the time. Even the single ones have noticed that you're more stressed than you were before he showed up. Is that the issue? Sex?" She glared at him, and he covered another bark of laughter with a cough. "Look, I'm trying to be delicate here. I didn't say he was going to pound you until your eyes rolled to the back of your head. Is that what you mean by saying you don't know what to do with him?"

"Marley Golden. What a thing to say to your mother. I should wash your mouth out with soap." He was right, though. That was the issue that she was having. "I'm not a virgin." He wisely said nothing. "I'm old, Marley. Thousands and thousands of years older than him. I know nothing about sex with someone that I'm going to see again in the morning. But it's not really the sex. It's being with him in that way. You know, as lovers." She growled. "I'm messing this all up."

"You're his friend, I'm guessing." She nodded and sat down again. "Do you talk about things? I mean, things that are going on around the Leap?

What you're going to be doing during the day while he—I just realized that I don't know what he does during the day while you're out and about."

"He's working in the barn with the equipment that is out there with his son. They're getting them cleaned up for winter. Also, he's fixing things that were damaged when being brought here by the movers. I tried to tell him that the faeries are willing to do it, but he wanted to do it himself." Marley asked if he was avoiding her too. She looked up at her son. "I never thought of it that way. I think he might be. He seems so on edge all the time. Like me, I guess."

"I would imagine that you both are. Just because you're mates doesn't make it so that everything is clear between the two of you. Does he have any idea what being mates means?" She said she didn't know if he understood that they were mates. "Perhaps that would be a good way for you to sit down and talk to him. He might not know or understand what is making him so frustrated all the time."

"I'll do it tonight." She was glad that he suggested talking to Tom. She'd spoken to him, and he did seem extremely frustrated all the time. "Now, what is this I hear about you boys building your own home? Is it true?" Marley looked shocked but only for a moment.

Then he smiled at her. She was glad that she knew about it so that she could have one up on her boys. It wasn't often that she could, but this time she was able to manage it. She asked if it was true that they were moving out.

"Yes. We think it would give you and Tom some privacy. And us as well. We were going to talk to you two about it tonight at dinner." She didn't say anything, but he could tell she was a little hurt. "It would do you some good, I think to have the house to yourself. Have you had any time alone here since your parents died?"

"No. Never. I've lived in this house with someone since they killed each other." She got up to get them some water. Morgan had a lot to think about. Things to put into order in her mind. Usually, she just knew what to say and when to say it, but this was personal. Nothing much that she had to deal with before. "Not long ago, I spoke to Tellus about you leaving me. I had it in my head that you'd literally leave me here and go off to parts unknown. She pointed out that all this land that they gave to me to work and to keep safe was for you guys to build a home on. You'd still be here where I needed you to be, but you'd also have a home, a residence all of your own. I should have told you then to build, but in the excitement of having the women around, I forgot. Do you suppose they'll not come over—I'm sounding whinny. I do believe they'll be here more than before when you build your homes. At least, that's my hope, anyway. But you mustn't bring people, outsiders here to build the homes, Marley. You make sure the others know that. The faeries have been wanting to build homes for you since you were tiny cubs."

"I think it would be faster anyway." She nodded, still distracted. "Our homes, at least mine, will be like here. Without anything that would ruin the earth that we have cherished here for so long. I don't believe that the others would do anything to harm their land either."

"I wouldn't think so. But you will have some things that I know that you have in your rooms now. Internet is one of the things. With children, I would think that it's important that they have that for school and such." He nodded. Before he could ask her what had her so upset, she turned and looked at him. "We'll still have dinners together, won't we? I don't mean nightly. I've only just thought of how much work that would be with all the children. I love them as much as I do you and your brothers. And the mates are just like ice cream on chocolate pie if you ask me." Marley laughed with her.

"Mom, you do know that you're the world to us. I don't care about this land or the trees and such here. Not nearly as much as I do you. It's you that I love. I would die for you." She told him that it would never come to that. "No. Perhaps not, but I want you to know that you are the only reason that all of us are who we are today. The only reason that our mates haven't killed us. You did such a good job in raising us. I can see that now. With the wives here, I can see that you did a job better than anyone else could have or would have. I love you with all my heart." She let the tears fall when he told her that. "We're going to get all mushy, aren't we?"

"Yes, but I find that I don't care." The door opened and closed behind her, and she nearly let go, but Marley hugged her tighter. When big strong arms wrapped around her from behind, she could smell that it was Carroll. "I love you boys so much."

She didn't know how long she'd been talking to Marley, but when Carroll said that he'd come over to talk to her about something, Morgan asked if it was about the houses. He looked at Marley, but he simply shook his head.

"I have friends in higher places than you can imagine. Or perhaps you can. I'm all for you all building yourself your own home. However, as I was telling Marley, the faeries need to be the ones that build it for you. They've been waiting for this moment for a very long time." Carroll asked if she was upset they were moving out. "I am. Don't get me wrong, I'm very upset, but it's time for you to be out on your own, and I'm happy for you all. You need your privacy as much as I do, and I'm thinking that it's well past the time for us to be a family that isn't around one another all the time. I'm sad but very happy for this next part of your lives. And mine too."

After they left, she made her way to the living room to wait for Tom. It was well beyond time that they talked to each other. He'd been staying here while his children settled up their affairs back home. Morgan was also glad that he seemed to be on board with the fact that they didn't use chemicals, and he loved the way that things worked so well on the compound. All in all, she was thrilled to have a man in her life after all this time. Surprising? Yes. But happy all the same.

Chapter 4

"Ms. Bander, where is your son, Cody Bander?" Melody didn't honestly know that he was missing until the police showed up, pounding on her door. Looking around the place that she'd managed to get from the government, she didn't see him. "We know that he's not here. Where is he so that we can speak to him? It's come to our attention that you've left him alone again to fend for himself. Where is he?"

"If you know so damned much, why don't you tell me where he is so that I can go and get him. Damn it, the fuck and back. Don't you have anything better to do than to annoy me at—what time is it anyway? Six in the morning?" He told her the time. And the date in the event, he said that she didn't know that either. "Eight at night? No, that can't be right. I was supposed to be going out, and I know I left him a note to—well, if he's not here, then he wouldn't have read it. Where is he? If his sister has come to get him, I'm going to be really pissed. She's not supposed to take him away from me, especially to another state."

"Ms. Bander is here as well. Last I heard, she was looking for him as well." Well shit. If Sin was here, then that meant that she knew that she'd left him to his own devices again. Melody should have left him some money this time. But that would have left her short on having enough for herself. And Melody thought of only herself. "Are you listening to me?"

"Not if I can help it. If you know where Sin is, then Cody is right there with her. She better not have left with him, or there will be hell to pay. I'm not shitting her this time. She ain't his mom. I am."

The cop asked her if she ever acted like either one of her children's mother. "Now that ain't none of your business, is it? I got us a nice home that we live in. And most of the time, there is food on the table. I'll have to be hitting up my daughter for some money for winter things for Cody."

"You did that already, Sin told us. That's why we figured you were gone. Did you spend it all on drugs and booze, Melody? Or did you gamble it all away?" He knew a great deal for not knowing where her boy was. Cody was her ticket to a lot of things, so she needed him here. "I'm speaking to you. Where is Cody?"

"How the hell do I know. He was here when I left him a couple of weeks—a couple of days ago. I was taking a nap, and he must have gotten out. I tell him over and over that, he can't just be running around like that. How will I know where he is?" The cop asked her if it was two weeks or two days. "You know that I've been warned about leaving him alone for two weeks. It was two days."

So, as soon as she got him back home, Melody

was going to make sure that he knew better than to involve the police or his sister. That shit was going to get her into trouble. She looked up at the officer, wondering why he was still here.

"You left him for four weeks this time, Melody. We know that because we have information that you spent a week of your time away in the jail down there. You've also been rousted twice for sleeping on the park benches and also trying to get into a library so that you could be warm. You also were part of a robbery at a donut shop just two days ago. We're still trying to figure out how you got away from that?" She was too. The fucking cops had nearly stepped on her twice when looking for her. "Since you don't seem to know where Cody is, I'll tell you. He's been staying with the Goldens out at Morgan's leap. I think that Sin is out there too. Might be hearing wedding bells soon, too, from what I've heard."

"You mean Sin might be marrying one of them men out there? Hot damn, that'll be good for me, don't you think?" The cop asked her how she figured it would have anything to do with her. "She's my daughter, ain't she? I mean, I'll be his mother-in-law, and he won't—which one is it? No, don't tell me, it doesn't matter. They're all rich as they can be. The guy will want his mother-in-law in the best situation so that he doesn't have to be ashamed of me. Damn, but that's the best news that I've heard all my life. When is the wedding? Can you take me out there to meet up with my future son? Christ, I could dance a jig. I'm so happy."

"I am not going to put you in my nice clean cruiser to smell it up. When was the last time you had a shower, Melody? You're stinky is what you are. Get a shower and clean up. You have a court hearing in the morning." She asked him for what. "I handed you the paperwork. If you want an attorney, then you should get there early to be assigned one."

"My son-in-law will make sure that I'm taken care of." Melody looked around for the paperwork and found it on the floor. After picking it up, she turned to the cop again to ask him if he'd wait on her to take her to her new home. But he was gone. "They take their time when you need one of them, but they're gone like a fart in the wind when you got a question for them. Bustards."

The woman across the street from her was standing in her driveway, staring at her. Flipping her off, Melody went into her house and put the paperwork on the counter. She didn't have any furniture to speak of. Not out here. But her bedroom was nice. The best mattress on the bed with silk sheets and the works. She even had herself some towels that were as fluffy as a dammed sheep. Yes, she had it all.

Needing to get ready to see Sin and her husband-to-be, she found her best dress, a red one, so that people would notice her to put on. After pulling it over her head, she was trapped in it long enough for her to realize that she did stink. Or it was the dress. Either way, she needed to get herself cleaned up a bit before she went to see them. Damn, but this was the best news yet. Even winning all that money for a few hours didn't compare to what she was going to do with all the money he was going to give her. And he would too. Or she'd spread rumors about him that would make him do what she said.

She scooped up all the good stuff all over her body. There was some kind of sparkly stuff, too, that she put in her hair when she rinsed it out. Stepping out of the shower, she realized that it felt really good to be cleaned up, and she did wonder why she didn't do it more often. Shaking her head, she found her dress just where she had left it and pulled it on again.

It was the dress that smelled, she realized. Melody had wasted her soap stuff for nothing. Spraying it with everything that she could put her hands on didn't make it smell any better, but she thought she could get by with wearing it one more time before she'd have to wash it. Not that she washed much of anything, Cody did that for her. But it would be cleaned when he returned. She was going to have him do her sheets too. In the event that Sin's future husband wanted a good roll in the bed for some extra cash for her.

It was nearly ten when she left home. The old bitty was still out there on her drive, watching her when she came out of the house. Waving at her, Melody asked her if her husband could give her a ride into town. She'd make it worth his while. But all she did was go into her house and slam the door.

"Must be losing my touch. Usually, I can get anyone to give me a ride someplace for a blow job." Then she remembered how far away she'd been from the woman and thought that was it. No way would her husband have turned her down.

Walking into town wasn't her idea of getting around, but as far as she knew, no one else in the development had a car. Or if they did, they kept it in the garage. She was going to have to go exploring to see what everyone had.

"I might even have to snatch myself a few things before I get things figured out." Since there was snow all over the place, she figured she'd have to get herself over to the mall soon. Putting Cody's name on that tree they had out for under privileged kids had given her quite a bit of money over the years. "I wonder if I can get by with putting Sin's name on there? I don't suppose anyone would care if I did or not. It's not like anyone pays for the shit that they give to my kid."

Melody was exhausted by the time she got to town. It must have been about fifty miles, it felt like. However, when she turned back to the way she'd come from, she could see not only the subdivision where she lived but also her house. She was going to have to get into better shape if she was going to be having some sex with the son-in-law. Just as she found herself a bench to sit down on, some woman appeared in front of her and smiled.

"Do I know you?" She said that she didn't. "Then get the fuck away from me. I've got shit to do, and you're not going to be helpful unless you have a car to drive me around in. I don't suppose you know who my daughter is marrying, do you? Sincerity Bander is her name."

"Marley Golden. But they're already married as of yesterday." The woman laughed. It wasn't a terrible laugh, but it was annoying to her. "The thought that you have in your head about having sex with him isn't going to fly. Not only would he be repulsed by you, but I think he might well cut his dick off rather than think of putting it anywhere near you. You smell like a whore."

"Well, ain't you just about the most pleasant person around. Not. I don't smell like a whore, dumb ass. Who are you anyway that thinks you can talk to me like that? I'm going to be his mother-in-law, and what's he going to think when I tell him what you called me?" She looked like she was thinking on it hard. Then she looked at her and said he'd only care that he didn't get to say it to her first. "Well, we'll see about that. I'll just have to take Sin from him if he gives me any shit. I'm guessing they have my son too?"

"Cody is a wonderful kid. Too bad that you're not more like him." Melody didn't understand if the woman was insulting her or not, so she let it go. "I was insulting you. And just for the record, my name is Veri Golden. I'm married to Marley's brother, Leslie. I'm also a witch."

"You're a bitch, that's for sure." The woman smiled at her. It wasn't really what she'd call friendly, but Melody didn't care. She had the upper hand in all this talking shit. "Why don't you take me to the house they're living in. I'm sure that he won't want me to be out on the streets this late at night."

"Really? I would think that you'd do more business out this late. That way, no one could really see what they're getting until it's too late." Melody didn't have any idea what the — then it occurred to her. "Good, I don't have to explain that one to you. How long do women your age work the streets before even the most desperate run from you? I would think that you're well past the age of wanting to get men to — "

"I can get any man I want. Women too." Veri just nodded, like she didn't believe a word she was saying. I can. You just watch and see that I can't. The next car that comes by here will be willing to pay me whatever I want to let him fuck me."

"The only people that are out this late, even for sex, aren't going to be coming down this street. That I can assure you, I'm put some magic around us so that we're not disturbed." Melody told her that she lied. "Of course, you would say that. I mean, you tell people that all the time when they tell you something that you don't want to hear. Like the man at the hotel that said you had to get out because the police were looking for you. You told him that he lied. He wasn't, by the way. Or the woman in the grocery store that you tried to steal some food from. She said that she had you on camera, and you said the same to her. She wasn't lying, either. The police from here to Vegas are looking for you. They have all kinds of videos of you robbing people. Killing them too. Mr. Graves, he died from his wounds when you took his wallet."

"I don't know what it is that you're talking about. If I *had* robbed someone for their wallet, they should have just handed it over when I asked him for it. I told him that I'd not hurt him if he did that." Veni said that he had handed it to her. "Well, not quick enough for me. And you know what? There was only twenty bucks in the fucker too. Who fights someone for twenty bucks?"

"He had several thousand dollars in his pocket. He'd only just cashed out his winnings for the night and was going home to his pretty wife and their new baby. The money in his wallet was a distraction. It worked, too, I guess. You didn't get the rest of his money. Now is wife is going to have to use a little of it to bury him. It's a shame, really. If you'd just kept yourself home like you were supposed to, then he would be alive and enjoying the winnings." She asked him how much he'd won. "One hundred and fifty grand. Enough to put them on easy street until they found themselves a better home."

"Damn bastard held out on me. How fair is that shit?" A car, a nice long limo, pulled up in front of the two of them. Melody had always wanted to ride around in one of them. Get off in one, too, but she'd never had the chance. The man and the woman that got out of it after having the door opened by the driver stared at the two of them. "Hey. You two got some cash on you that I can have? I'm trying to get to the Golden place where my family is. I don't suppose you'd let me borrow that thing for a—"

"Hello, Mom. Christ, what the fuck are you wearing?" Melody had to squint to see who the woman was and realized that it was Sin. She asked her where she was headed. "Veri contacted us and told us what you were thinking. You're not going to be welcome in our home, Mom. Not ever. Nor will you ever take Cody away from me again. I'm adopting him with Marley."

Melody eyed the big man. He was big too. Broad across the shoulders. Taller than a tree, she thought. She'd bet anything that he had a dick as long as her arm. She thought that she could have some fun riding the man. And his clothing looked like he'd stepped right out of one of them manly mags where men posed in their underwear. The man laughed, and she looked at him.

"I can read your mind. You'll never touch me in that way so that's nothing you have to worry about. And Sin is right on both accounts. You're not going to be welcome anywhere in town so long as I'm breathing. And that's going to be a good deal longer than you will be." She told him that they'd see about that. "You go on thinking that. And while you're at it, you should know that we've pressed charges against you for child abandonment. The police are looking for you right now."

As if he had some sort of pull, they pulled up behind the limo with their lights flashing. She was ready to take off running when something hit her hard in the chest. Piss ran down her legs as she was tazed. Christ, she thought, she was going to smell really bad after this.

~*~

Tom wasn't sure what to make of the information that he'd been given. While he knew what mates were, it was still something that he wasn't sure that he believed in. But he had fallen in love with Morgan in a very short amount of time, and he was positive that he could easily spend the rest of his life with her.

"You'll live forever too." He put up his hand, and she had to laugh. "I'm sorry. I think that each of the women in this family did the same thing. I'm sorry that I'm overwhelming you. But I'd never lie to you about anything that you ask me."

"What do you mean, forever? I mean, I'm to understand that you're older than me, but just how much are you older?" She told him that he'd never die. Nor would his children or any children that they had. "And the second question? I have a feeling that I'm not going to take it any better than I did living forever, am I?"

"More than likely not. I've been around for thousands of years." He nodded, not sure what to think about that. "I'm also the queen of all shifters. The boys, my sons, they're the first shifters ever created. I suppose that would make you the king of all shifters too. I'll have to ask Tellus about that."

"Tellus? I know my history well enough to know that Tellus is supposed to be some kind of terrestrial being that cares for the earth. Roman, I think that is." She said that she was real too. "I see. No, I don't, but I'm working on it. Who else do you know that I might well have heard of? Give it to me slowly. I beg of you."

"They're here now. All of my friends. Joel is in the kitchen making tea. Then there is Thad. He's retiring soon. The king of all Gnomes." He only nodded again. Feeling like he was on a three-day bender and not sure which way was up. "I can't explain things to you if you don't want to listen to me."

"I'm trying. I really am." She nodded just as a pretty woman appeared in the room. Tom could only stare at her. She was pretty, but she was also very sparkly. And she had wings. "You must be Tellus. I've read stories about your great magic. You'll have to forgive me. I'm running on empty right now, trying to get things straight in my head."

"You're doing just fine, Tom. I'm so happy to finally get to meet you. And yes, I'm Tellus. Joel is coming as well. He's raiding the cookie tin that Morgan has for us. Also, there is David. I won't overwhelm you any more about what he is. Thad is just there on the end of the couch. You can see him, correct?" The little man tipped his hat at him and welcomed him to the family. "When Morgan told us who you were to her, you cannot believe how excited we all were for the two of you. And you have children of your own. That's so lovely. They'll live forever too. As well as any children that you and

Morgan might have."

"Children? I have grown children now. I'm a tad bit too old to be having more, don't you think?" Tellus told him that he was as magical as Morgan was as well as the king of all shifters. Morgan told Tellus that she wasn't helping. "I need a minute here. Just…things are going too fast for me."

"I understand." A man with a large tin came into the room. Behind him were faeries, who he had met already. They were carrying cups of tea as well as glasses of what looked like some kind of juice. Morgan handed him a glass of the amber colored liquid. "You need to drink this. It's only apple juice, but it'll help you with your magic. Also, have some cookies. They'll be good for you as well."

He found that he did feel better after drinking down the glass of juice, but when it refilled itself, he sat it down on the coffee table. Tom noticed that his hands were shaking. He looked around the room. There were a lot of people in the room with him and Morgan. They were quiet for the most part, but that didn't make him feel any less overwhelmed by it all.

It wasn't until Marley came into the room that he felt like he'd been handed a lifeline. Taking his hand into his, he told him what was going on.

"Mom called for me when she thought you were going to lose your shit. Are you?" Tom told him that he thought perhaps he'd already lost it. "Yes, I can see that. There is too much going on in your mind for me to search for what is bothering you the most. But if you were to take a deep breath, I'll try and explain what I can for you. What is the first thing that pops into your head?"

"Living forever." Marley nodded and smiled. "I don't know why that is there, but it is. I'm not sure that I want to live forever. I wouldn't even—I know that you're all old, but I don't understand this."

"When my mother, Morgan, was just a child, her parents sold her to some nasty men that were to rape then kill her. If not for the large leopard that was out and about looking for food, they might well have succeeded. As it turned out, Mom brought the leopard home, here and took care of her. And her kittens. Years later, Golden eyes, who is my biological mother, called to mother earth and asked her to take care that her children, my brothers and I were able to make it in the world." Tom didn't know what this had to do with him living forever, but he was feeling calmer by the story. "We became the first shifters of the world. And have since gone around and helped other shifters, ones that we had a hand in creating, were able to blend into the world of humans so that they'd not be killed. Morgan was gifted forever as well as we were so that we could take care of the world around us and beyond."

"How long ago was this? She said thousands of years, but I have a feeling that it's longer than that." Marley said that they'd been around long enough to have been able to see cars being made. Electricity in homes as well as plumbing. "That's not so long ago, son. What are you trying hard not to tell me? Please, I'm feeling a little better now, and I think that I could handle it."

"When we were born, Julius Caesar was a ruler of his country, Rome. He died in forty-four BC by being stabbed to death when magic was given to the earth here so that we could live on this land on our own. My family was here, in this country, trying to get as much as we could from the earth." Tom said that wasn't possible. "Not only is it possible, but it's also as true as anything that you've been told so far. While everything was going on in that country, we were here, living in our own world, trying to gouge out a living by turning the earth. We've seen ships coming in with goods. Bringing not just stables that we'd had for decades but also people that settled around the area too. We've lived here, working the land and surviving on it since well before there were people here living in homes. Mom's parents had come here with the intent to take over this country and rule it as their own. The very balcony that they fell to their deaths from wasn't really a balcony but more of a ledge that wasn't meant to hold people. The story that we tell has been modified so that people, people like you, would be able to believe it."

"I don't know what to believe, to be honest with you." Tom didn't either. He was looking around the room, noticing things that he'd never seen before. Or, more than likely, hadn't wanted to see. He stood up to look at the armor that was standing by the fireplace that looked like it might well have been used during Caesar's time. "This is real, isn't it?"

"Yes. None of us ever wore it, but it is from the same time as Pompey and Crassus. It was brought here one night to show what sort of stupidity was being done across the world. I think it might have been Joel who brought it here for us to see." Joel nodded and said that he still thinks it silly that they fought so many wars. "There are other things here if you wish to look around. Swords from wars. Bows and arrows that were used by the first Indians that lived around here. Mom took in as many of the horses as she could do save them. But no man or woman had ever been able to make their way here to this land. It was and still is a sacred place for the earth to heal and to grow. No wars were fought on these lands simply because of all the magic that is here."

Tom did wander around the room. He was seeing things that he'd not seen before. There were swords in corners that had been labeled as to where they'd been found. A long line of shells from different places were there to see. Picking one of them up, he was surprised by how big it was and put it back when he got a small glimpse of the death that it had caused.

Putting his hands behind his back, when he picked up a long bejeweled knife and saw that it was used to kill a woman in her bridal gown, Tom decided not to touch anything else. Coming back around the room, he sat down next to Morgan and took her hand into his. After telling her what he'd experienced, she kissed him on the cheek and told him that she could do the same. While it was good to know he wasn't off his noodle, he was nervous about how real the images were to him.

He noticed that the others were talking and enjoying the cookies in the tin. He would have thought that by now it would have been emptied but realized that it was much like his glass of juice, never-ending. Occasionally he would ask a question, and the answer was given to him. But as time moved on, Tom realized that he was all right with everything that was being said to him. Not only that, but he came to realize that he was in love with Morgan and couldn't wait to get to know her better.

His children, as well as Morgan's, had come home for dinner. It was, he thought, one of the most enjoyable things that they did as a family. Coming together to talk to each other and to go over some of the things that they'd done today. Even with him working around equipment older than he was, he enjoyed hearing that his boys were having a wonderful time as well. Even his daughter, who had had a bad ending to her marriage, seemed to be thrilled to be hanging out with all of them nightly. It was something that Tom could get used to, he thought.

After dinner, while the sun was still shining, he and Morgan took a walk around the compound. It was much larger than he thought, but it was run like a well ran company. Even the way that the gardens were rotated around, it seemed like something that they were good at. Tom supposed that after all this time, it would be like second nature to have it running so well. He was glad too to find out that he could have fresh fruit and vegetables year round as well as anything else his heart desired. Yes, Tom thought, he was well on his way to falling in love with this place as much as he loved Morgan. And he did, he finally realized. He loved Morgan so much more than he did his first wife. Happy now, Tom pulled Morgan into his arms for a much-needed kiss. She was wonderful, and he was happy beyond words to be able to call her his.

Chapter 5

Connie was about as ready as she ever was going to be to face the fucking witch that dared defy her. Instead of calling out to Zippy—a ludicrous name if there ever was one—Connie sat in the middle of her circle and called to the other beings around her. It was time that she made good on her threats and pulled their magic for her own.

Being as strong as she was, Connie thought for sure that the magic would have filled her immediately. Feeling some resistance, she dug her magic deeper into the spell she was casting and felt some of the magic come to her. However, it didn't feel right. Like she was missing some vital part of it.

"You are missing a great deal of magic, as it so happens." Opening one eye, she looked at the being sitting on the outside of her circle and told him to go away. "I'm afraid that's not going to work for me. You're the one that disturbed my rest, so you're going to have to deal with me. You're Constance Jamison, aren't you? We in the magic world just refer to you as Nine Finger. I think that it suits you quite well."

"You will not insult me with that name. I'm Connie, grand witch of all witches." The being tisked. "I am. I only have one person that I have to take care of, and I'll be the richest woman in the world."

"No, I've met the grand witch. And her sister. You're neither of them. However, I do have some advice for you if you'd like to take it. I'd steer clear of them both. They work well together, and they have a familiar now. He's going to be crowned Grand warlock soon too." Connie said that she'd be the one to decide who was the grand warlock. "You think so, do you? Well, I'm guessing that you're off your rocker if you think that saying something like that is going to make it true. It's not, in case you're wondering. You didn't ask me who I am. You should have. It's very rude of you to not—"

"I don't give a flying fuck who you are. Just get out of here." The being, a large man who she'd didn't believe for a minute, was magical, snapped his fingers, and not only did he have a chair that looked comfy but also a large drink and a plate of cookies. "Morgan gives me a tin of these when I visit her. Just the other day, she met her mate. Wonderful thing to have someone to spend their life with. Tom is a wonderful person. I think that you'd like him if you weren't such a terrible person. Speaking of which, I've spoken to Zippy and Veni, and they told me to tell you that they'll be by soon. What is this place you're living in anyway?"

"It's an abandoned barn. It was all I was left with when my mother was given all that I had. She made them think that it was her home when it was mine. I'm the stronger of the two of us. Everything I want should be coming to me. But that bitch, Zippy, not only kicked me from my home, but she also made it so that I can't walk on the earth around the house too."

"That doesn't sound like you're all that particularly strong. How are you going to take on the two women if you can't even make your mother do what you want? I think you should think on that a bit before the lovely Golden women get here. They'll turn you into something horrendous if you don't watch yourself." He thought about it a moment. "Do witches do that still? Turn people they don't care for into toads and whatnot? I love what the smaller creatures like toads and worms do to the earth. They're so vital to everything that goes on. Well, every creature is, but I love the toads and worms."

"Yes, especially annoying men who come around where they're not wanted." He pointed out again that she had woke him. "Yes, so you said. You were taking a rest of something."

"It was a good rest, too, but you woke me up. But it's fun to hang out with you. My name is Joel, by the way. I'm the king of the trees. I've been around for a good long time, and I'm only just enjoying my time on earth of late. Morgan and her family are growing, you see, and then there is Sammy. He's going to be the King of all Gnomes soon."

"King of Gnomes? Are you mad? There is no such thing as a king of gnomes. Those little creatures that are put in gardens as decoration, those sorts of creatures?" Joel told her that they looked nothing like the little beings that humans put in their gardens. "Sure they don't. Then I have to wonder why they look like they do? Like some long-bearded person with a hat on. You can't even see their eyes."

"Thad has beautiful blue eyes. His hair is dark, though, at times, it looks like fall. I'll have to ask him that before he retires if his hair goes along with the seasons." Connie screamed. It was the only way to get some people to shut up. "I don't need all that noise, you know. Just ask me politely to tone it down, and I will. Would you like a cookie? They're very good."

"No, I don't want a cookie. What grown man sits around and eats cookies anyway? I don't want you here either. Why don't you get up off your ass and leave me the fuck alone." He tisked at her again. "Why are you even here? Other than you claiming that I woke you up. Why are you hanging around here when I'm sure that as king of bushes, you have shit to do."

"King of Trees. I supposed bushes, too, but king of trees is my official title. And perhaps if you were to eat some cookies yourself, you might be in a better disposition than you are now. Crabby and rude is all that you are." She growled at him. "There you go. That just proves my point about you being crabby. Who growls at people? No one does unless they're going to attack. Marley does that. But when he does it, I'm sure that someone is going to get their butt handed to them. He could do it too. Ah, here they are. Zippy, you look lovely today. And Veni, a beauty too. She's all yours. But I'd be careful with her. She has it in her head that she's all-powerful when she was only able to wake me when she was reaching out for magic. Had it not woke up my son when he was napping, I might not have noticed. But she did make the trees laugh, so they woke him up, so that can't be all bad."

The man disappeared when the two women pulled chairs from nothing and sat down on them. They were going on and on about the baby, the son of Joel, when she'd had enough. Telling them to shut the fuck up, Zippy snapped her fingers, and her mouth disappeared. Connie tried every reverse spell she knew, and it wouldn't bring her mouth back.

"You did tell me she was full of herself. Christ, she is annoying as hell. How is it that you let her go the first time?" Zippy explained to who Connie thought was Veni. She could feel their power, but it didn't bother her any. There were others that she'd taken magic from that were much stronger. As they were talking about whatever suited them, Connie tried to calm herself. Being pissed off would make her make mistakes, and she was much too strong to let a little anger through her off. "Are you ready to get this over with, Nine Fingers?"

With another snap, her mouth was back. But as soon as she opened her mouth to blast the two of them, a squeaky voice came out. As both of the other two laughed at her mousy voice, Connie had to work ten times harder to get her voice back the way it had been. It still squeaked but not as badly as before.

"I'm the grand witch of all witches. You will heed my—" Veni cut her off, telling her that she wasn't saying it with enough authority. That her voice needed to be deeper. Connie found herself nodding and trying again. "I'm the grand witch of all witches. You will heed my power so that I can take all your power."

"You're not suppose to announce what you're going to do, dumbass. And for as long as it takes for you to say all that, you're going to be toast. Just do your thing and get it over with." Connie had to breathe in and out before she could speak again. "Also, You're using the word power too much. I'm sure there are plenty of other words you could use instead of power."

"Oh yes. I know a few. Energy. I'm not sure that would work in this instance, but it is a good word. Then there is control and force." Zippy said a couple more words before Veni laughed. "Those are all good replacements. Try any of those, Nine Finger. I personally like—"

"Will you two shut the fuck up?" Christ, Connie thought. It was like being in a bad television show or something. "I'll say what I want, and you'll do as your told."

"I don't think so. I believe that we've fucked around long enough with you. How about we just judge and sentence you now so that we can go back to our mates and have an enjoyable evening. You're not all that much fun anyway. What do you think, Zippy?" Zippy said it was funny when she got all blustery mad at them. "Oh, well, yes, there is that."

Before she could say another word, she was suddenly in a grand room with people there that she didn't know. Veni was sitting high on a dais while her sister was standing in front of her. Connie didn't know what was going on, but she had a feeling that she might well have bitten off more than she could chew right now. She wanted to regroup and rethink what she needed to do.

"I think you've had more than enough time to do that. Your hand is nicely healed. Though I'm to understand that it does give you fits every once in a while. But that's me. I don't want you to get too uppity before this trial." She asked Zippy what she was talking about. "The trial that you're going to be sentenced in. I'm sure you were told. I did send out a letter to you several times. Didn't you get them? I'm sure you did."

"You mean those silly notes about when to be ready for my day in court. I didn't bother with them as I have more important things to do." Zippy told her that she should have gotten ready as this was life or death for her. "You have no rights to kill me. Or anyway that you can, for that matter. I'm a grand witch, and I'm going to be the most powerful witch in the world."

"I thought that once you achieved being a grand witch, you were all powerful?. So which is it? You *are* the grand witch with all the power, or you're going to be a grand witch with all the power?" Connie said that as soon as she killed her, she'd be powerful. "Oh, well, that makes more sense. However, I'd not look for it to be easy for you. Not even obtainable either if you want to know the truth. I'm sister to the real grand witch, and you're nothing but a two-bit witch that hasn't the magic to call up anything to help you today."

"I don't need anyone's help." Zippy asked her if she was sure about that. "I am. I have enough power right now to take you on and come out on top."

"Go ahead. Give it your best shot. We'll all wait, won't we?" The people in the room with them nodded, telling her that she had this. Reaching out to pull all the magic to her, she was surprised by the lack of magic in the room. "Oh, I did forget to tell you. All the people here are dead. By your hand, as it turns out. You can't retake their magic since you've killed them for their own. Lesser witches, too, that had less power than you do. That's a punishable by death rule that you broke over two hundred times, Nine Fingers."

"My name is Connie, Grand Witch of all

Witches." Her anger made her spill a little of her magic on the ground. Trying to gather it back to her, she watched as it made its way to the people with them. "What the hell is going on here? What the hell are you doing to me? You can't drain my magic. You said yourself that it's a rule that you can't take from lesser witches. What do you think you're doing now?"

"But you've been telling us for the past hour that you're the grand witch. Haven't you?" Connie nodded, not at all sure what was going to happen to her when more of her magic spilled out on the floor beneath her. "As you have noticed, more and more of your ill-gotten magic is going to its rightful owners. While it won't bring them back from death, they will be able to share it with novice witches. Ones that they want to share with. Not you, I guess, since it's leaving you like rats on a sinking ship."

"I demand that you give me my due." Zippy looked at the dais and then back at her. "Do you have to have it cleared by your big sister, Zippy? Oh, how sad for you. You must be so jealous of her magic."

"Not really. She has gifted me a great deal of power. I can do this." Connie felt the magic that she had that kept her beautiful stripped from her body. Falling to her knees, she didn't look up so that others could see her face. "My goodness. You're not supposed to use your magic for your own gain, either. I guess I missed that one. Oh well. I can do this as well."

Each time she moved her hands in front of her, Connie felt more and more of her being stripped away. Not just the magic that had kept her young for so long but also the magic that had kept her in good shape. Kept her from being ill, and her bones mended. As she curled into a heap on the floor, she saw her mother there. Looking younger than she'd ever looked in her life.

"How?" Mother seemed to understand and got down on her knees to speak to her. "How? Beautiful?"

"I was gifted this from Veni for helping her with your trial. I gave her your spell book, too, along with the names of the witches that you harmed. It wasn't as difficult as I thought it would be, turning my only child out. But with the way that you've treated me over the years, I found it to be quite easy and even rewarding to not have to worry about how badly you were going to beat me again. Not to mention, it's nice knowing that I have something to eat all the time as well." Mother stood up. "Goodbye, Nine Fingers. I do hope you enjoy the life that they've set aside for you."

Connie found herself sitting in a chair in an over the top floral room. The bed was small, nothing like she usually slept in. The walls were covered in rose and carnation paper. Even the curtains on the windows were covered in the same sickening design. It was Zippy that spoke to her from somewhere in the room about her new life.

"You're to spend the rest of your days in this nursing home. You'll be cared for much better than you did your mother and grandmother, but not too much more. There will be someone to come in and feed you. Someone will come in and change your diaper and clothing as well." Connie tried to tell her that she was going to get her for this. "Yeah, not going to happen. I'll come and check on your occasionally. Tell you what's going on around you. Not that you'll be able to participate in any of it, but I'll let you know about it. Also, you'll be here a good deal longer than most of the residents too. You'll be here for the next fifty years, Nine Fingers. I do hope you have a good time."

When she was left alone, she could hear the other people yelling at one another about some kind of game. A nurse came in, she told her that her name was Nurse Sally and that she'd be caring for her tonight. No matter how much she screamed at the people around her, no one could hear her. But in the back of her mind, she could hear Zippy. Singing and laughing about the next fifty years or so.

This wasn't right. There was no way that they'd leave her here. Calling for Zippy to come back, she was left with laughter. Singing again and laughing. It wasn't until she was being fed her lunch that she realized the song she was singing to her was about a lovely bunch of coconuts. Over and over again.

~*~

Sin was excited about their new home. The faeries had asked her and Marley all kinds of questions about what they wanted. How big they wanted the home too. Lots of bedrooms, they had told Button. He was in charge of talking to the construction crew of faeries that was going to build their home. There were other groups for the other homes that would be going up today as well. However, right now, she had to focus on the job at hand. Coming out with a spring catalog.

So here she was. Instead of watching her home go up, she was in her new building. Staring at the mannequin, she wondered why it had looked so amazing at home, but here, in this new life, it didn't suit her thoughts on colors or fabric at all.

"Mistress, the others and I were wondering if you were going to need the scraps on the floor about. There is a large box of them as well that we packed to bring here as well." She asked Donut what they would do with them. "Oh, mistress, we can do so much with a bit of cloth. Make clothing for ourselves. Then there are blankets and curtains. I heard that one of the women in the colony is going to make up blankets for the wee little ones that are born to us. I think that will be most grand."

"I guess I never thought that you'd have to make things for yourself. You're so generous to all of us with your magic." He explained to her that rule about not being able to use one's magic to make their life better. "Surely that doesn't mean warm clothing and curtains."

"I'm afraid it does." She smiled at Veni and asked her what she thought of the dress on the mannequin. "Honestly? I think you can do better. And why are you using silk in the spring? I've seen your line recently for fall. While I'd love to own a couple of the dresses, there isn't really any place that I could wear them. But those colors remind me more of winter than spring. What's going on here?"

"I'm not sure. I've been in here four times over the last five days, and I can't think of what I'd been thinking about when I designed this dress. I mean, I love the cut and the way that it hangs. But I can't get past the fact that it is ugly. There I said it, it's ugly."

They both laughed. "I was talking to Donut about the scraps of material. I have it in my head now to do something for them. I find I love living a life of leisure. Such as it is. I think I work harder now as a part of this place than I ever did back home."

"Me too. All I did was hang low so that no one would understand that I was a witch. I don't have that issue here. Even with the people in town. They've accepted me right away." She went to the dress, and the color on the clothing turned white. "A fresh start. I'm guessing that you know what the new colors are going to be for spring. So what are they?"

"You know, I usually do, but I've not paid any attention since I've been here. It's like it doesn't mean as much to me as it used to." She watched as the faeries and the brownies were going through the box of scraps. Their excitement was contagious. Going to where they were, she dumped the box on the table so that they could get to more colors. "Perhaps I can do something like this. Help out with scraps and such."

"I don't know that you'd want to just cut up a bunch of these colors just for the faeries, Sin. That will surely eat up any kind of money that you might have had. What if you were to make blankets with the material. Like for nursing homes and shut-ins?" Sin looked at Veni, and she knew she could tell that she was excited. "They are forever needing things like blankets and other items. I know for a fact that blankets, warm ones, are high on their list of things to be donated, even in the shelter. Sometimes people come into the place with nothing more than the clothing on their backs. It would be nice of you to be able to supply them with blankets to use."

"I'm going to do it." Stripping the clothing off the mannequin, Sin began pulling material off the shelves that she had only just put up. "They wouldn't have to be fancy or anything. I'd make them with love, of course, but they'd not have to be anything that would match their rooms. Quilts are to be crazy, right?"

"You should have Morgan come in and tell you how to get started on making quilts. I know that the ones on the boys' beds are ones that she made from their old clothing. This was before they figured out that they could make their own clothing. Now she just goes down to the thrift store and purchases all the things they have at the end of the month. It's a win-win for everyone." Within an hour, Sin had a design made up of what she wanted. No, they'd not have to be fancy, made of silks and such, but they'd have designs on them that would make the person receiving them happy. At least, she hoped.

"May I help, Mistress? The others and I, we'd like to have a way of thanking you for the material. And making blankets for the elderly is something that we'd love to be a part of." She showed him the design that she wanted to create, and in less time than it took her to draw it out, she was looking at the finished product. "Oh my. Oh my. This is so beautiful. I will have to make myself one like this one. This is so warm looking too."

The log cabin was in the middle of a deep and dark forest. The trees were nearly bare now with the onset of the colder months. Smoke came from the chimney, and there were leaves all over the ground. Sin thought that when she ran her finger over them, she could hear them crunch. There were animals in the woods, some that she'd not thought of in her design, but with the faeries' help, she could see where they were enjoying the last of the grass and flowers that were there. Every time she looked at it, she could see something else, some other thing that she knew wasn't a part of the overall design. The butterfly, up in the left corner, was her favorite thing. It even had her signature on it. Just Sincerity.

"Mistress, if you were to allow us to help you in the endeavor, we would be grateful. It's allowing us to show others, the elderly and whatnot, something that I know they miss. The outdoors. Such as a deer in their yard. A squirrel running up the trees. Yes, it would be such a change for us other than planting flowers that I would find them so relaxing to do." She said that she'd have to ask Morgan and Tellus. "Oh yes. They'll be so happy to have us working all the time that they'd be thrilled that this will be helping those in town. Oh my, this will be such a good thing for us little people to do."

She was going to enjoy it even if she couldn't

have the help of the little people. Morgan showed up with Button, her faerie, and they talked about how much it would help the townspeople. Tellus was all for it so long as they were paid a wage.

It took Sin a few minutes to realize that she'd not have to give them money — watching them pull a quarter along behind her sent her into giggles until Tellus told her that the scraps would be the perfect payment. She knew that she'd find that funny, Donut carrying around a wallet that was bigger than him to cash his check. Then her mind went to him having a driver's license, and she nearly lost her mind laughing and trying to explain to the two women what had her laughing so hard. She was losing her mind, and it was only eight in the morning.

In the end, she was able to use the faeries and brownies so long as they wanted to work with her. She was sure she'd have to put things off until word got around about the blankets and who would want to help, but she was all right with that too. So long as she could get one done a week, she would be happy to have someone else using them. She said as much to Morgan.

"You don't think that anyone will want to make blankets with you?" Sin told Morgan that it would be all right if they didn't. She knew how to make them. "Sin, you're going to have so many of the little people working with you that you're going to have to close down a couple of days a week because there will be so many blankets made. And I'm betting right now that there are some of them coming up with designs to help you out. They'll be beautiful as well, but I'm thinking you're going to be very busy."

"You really think so?" Morgan just pointed to the ceiling of her building at the thousands of faeries up there. "I never thought...well, obviously, I didn't think they'd want to help. At this rate, I'll run out of material before we're even getting started." She told her that the company that they own that helps with donations would supply her with the material. "Oh no, I wouldn't want to—"

"Sin, this is what we do. We help those in need. And I think this is one of the better things that have come from this leap in a long time. Something that they can hold onto and love while it keeps them ever so warm. Yes, this is a wonderful idea." Thanking the other woman, she hugged her. "I needed that too. What do you say that we get the little people started on at least a hundred blankets. Tell them a number, or you'll not be able to enter this room when you come back because they will fill this place up in no time. Tell them the size as well as where to put them when they are finished."

"I have noticed that without direction, they can go a bit overboard." They were still laughing when Donut asked her if she had a moment. Going to the design room with him, she wasn't the least bit surprised to find that there were designs drawn on the walls, floors as well as the ceiling. Clearing her throat, she told them what she wanted them to do for the people in town. "Make me only one hundred blankets for today. That way, if no one wants them, we won't be stuck with too many. Also, I'd like for you to stack them neatly on the shelves over there. Tomorrow we'll figure out how to package them up so that we're not overwhelmed when we send them out."

After giving them the sizes she wanted, Morgan had had to make a call to the local nursing home to see what sort of beds they used, and that gave them something to work with. They used mostly full beds, but they did have a few singles as well. Right now, they only had fifty-one residents. That, too, was a number that they could work with, to begin with. Morgan also made it clear that the blankets belonged to the residents, and if they wished, they could take them with them when they left.

"You mean die." Morgan nodded. "I guess I never let myself think beyond keeping them warm while alive. But perhaps a family member will want to keep it for a remembrance. I think, even if they don't, I want to think that they will. All right?"

"Yes. All right. Now, let's go and see your new house go up. I've had them waiting on you until you were ready. You are ready, correct?" She said that she was. "Good. We'll make our way there and see it going up for the two of you. I was sort of sad that my boys were moving out of the big house, but I'm so happy now that they'll be living so close to us yet far enough away that they can do whatever it is they wish."

She was happy about that too. Sin was going to enjoy decorating her own home. She'd given it very little thought before because she was so happy to have Marley in her life, but to have their own space, out in the open, was going to be epic for them. And their children if they decided to have any. Life was so exciting right now, and she couldn't have been happier with the way things had turned out.

Chapter 6

Sammy was learning as much as he could from the elderly gnome. Thad had been his first friend when they arrived here several months ago. Now that he was going to retire, it was left up to Sammy to take over Thad's job and do right by his honor of choosing him to be the one that would be king of all gnomes.

"I've had me a word or two with Tellus. She's a hoot, don't you think?" Sammy was distracted and just nodded at his friend. He'd been trying for two days now to make sure that he knew how to use this particular bit of magic, and it wasn't coming to him as easily as the other had. "Sammy, you're thinking too hard, son. Just think about the water and where you want it to go, and it'll do it. Come on now. Just wish it sort of like to go to the ditch that we've had built."

"What am I supposed to do if this doesn't work? Am I going to have to bring it over to the ditch a bucket at a time?" He'd been nasty and rude, and as soon as the words left his mouth, Sammy sat down and cried. "I'm messing up everything. I'm working so hard on trying to make you proud of me that I can't get this one thing to work like I need it to. I'm a failure."

"Now, don't you be saying something like that, young Sammy. You're never a failure unless you stop trying. You're going to get it. You're just a tad stressed out. Sit like I told you. That's it. Sit so that you can lean back against Mr. Tree here, and we'll have us a nice rest. I'm feeling I need a nap myself. Now, are you situated nicely?" Sammy said that he was but had to shake off a bit more of the stress that he was feeling before he was able to lie back against the tree and let his body relax by degrees. "I can hear the tree singing to me. I needed that too."

"Of course you did. I did as well. Is he singing you the winter is coming song? That's one of my favorites. They'll be so lovely in the spring after they close their body up for the winter. Yes siree bob, it'll be a sight to see when they come back in the spring. Not that I don't enjoy the fall, but the spring, when all the little flowers are coming out to be pollinated, is a sight that keeps me having hope for us all. There you go. You're not at all stressed out, are you?"

"No. Even my headache isn't as bad." Thad told him he was too young to be letting his headache make him cranky. "I know. I shouldn't have taken it out on you, either. Thank you, Thad. This is just what I needed."

With his eyes closed and his head resting where it was, he was feeling better. Sammy hadn't been sleeping all that well. He was forever worried about messing up so that there was no more gnome magic in the world. Mostly he was terrified of being alone. Once Thad left him, he'd not have a friend.

Sammy knew he was much too shy when he went to school. Smart too. The other kids hated that he was so smart. Not that he held it over them or anything. It was the teacher that would make it known that he'd passed the test with perfect scores. He supposed that he could get his mom or dad to have a word or two with them, but he was set up to be a ruler. Shouldn't he be able to handle some kids treating him like he was dirt?

Last week he'd been bullied to the point of crying. One thing you did not do when you're being a target was cry, he'd figured out. That only made things ten times worse for you. But he'd gotten hurt, and once his tears started, he couldn't have stopped them for any amount of money.

"You show that sore place on your arm to your momma?" He told him that he'd not. But it was getting better every day. "I'm sure it is, son, but you have to tell her. They didn't break your arm this time, but they might the next. Then where will you be?"

"She'll go in there with guns blazing." Thad laughed when he did. "I can almost see her doing that now. She'll head right to the office and tear into the secretary about it. Then the principal. My goodness, they'll say that Golden woman sure does love her kids. And I know she does, but I will be worse off if she does anything at all."

"I know that I don't have to tell you this, but don't you be using your magic on them. That'll be bad for everyone." Sammy told Thad that he wished they had a magical school for kids. So that everyone would be magical and no one would be different. "They'd find something different about you. It doesn't matter where you are or how much you're careful. Kids will be bullies because they were more than likely bullied at home. Not all, but there are some out there."

Sammy agreed with Thad but didn't move from his space. Not even talking about being bullied right now was making him stressed again. He was safe. He knew that more than he knew what they were having for dinner tonight.

"I've been talking to the lady queen about me

leaving you. And how much it hurts me." He said that he didn't want to talk about it right now. "All right. That's good. But I will tell you that she said that I didn't have to leave. But you go on resting. I don't think you've been resting all that—"

Sammy bolted upright and turned to his friend. His excitement was barely contained. "What did you say?" Thad winked at him and said that he didn't have to die when he took over. "Ever? You can stay with me forever?"

"I can't help you, you know. I won't have that kind of magic anymore. You understand that about two very strong beings occupying the same space, right?" Sammy said that he did. His smile stretched from ear to ear. "Well, I'd be there with you as your friend. I can advise you on things, little things, but I can't tell you what I'd do. If I do, then I have to die. But I can help you. Just not do it for you. You are my friend, Sammy. My dearest friend. I find I just can't leave you, or my heart will be forever broken."

"Mine too." They were both sobbing then. Thad let him pick him up, and he held him to his heart. "That's why I'm stressing all the time. I don't have any friends at all but for you. I don't count my family. But you? You're all I have in the world, Thad."

They were both sobbing out their happiness of being together. Thad explained to him again how he could only give advice, and Sammy was all right with that. They were both so giddy in their happiness that they failed to hear his dad walking up on them.

"I see you got the—what happened to your arm, Sammy? Did you fall?" It was on the tip of his tongue to tell his dad that he had fallen. However, one look from Thad, and he found that he couldn't do it. He loved his dad and thought he'd be less likely to go to the school with a gun than his mom would have.

After explaining to him what had been happening, his dad asked him why he'd not told them. Sammy and Thad both told him about how they were afraid that his mom would go in there and hurt someone if they went to her. She was protective of them like a bear.

"Yes, well, she is at that. But we'll have to tell her, you know. She won't be happy if we go in there without her." Sammy nodded but didn't tell him that he was afraid of his mom at times. "She scared me to death at times. I love her to pieces, and I know that she'd never hurt any of us, but you were right in describing her like a bear with her cubs. My goodness, I'd feel sorry for the boys more than the teacher. Unless she knows it's going on."

"She does. Mrs. Mann told me that I had to learn to stand up for myself, or I'll never get anywhere in this world. I didn't tell her that I was going to go further than she was. Anyway, she watches them beat the snot out of me. Sometimes she even tells them that they're doing a good job in making me a better man than my dad is. I had to figure out that she meant you, not the other one."

"Mrs. Mann needs to watch what she's saying, I'm thinking." Dad said that he was going to ask his mom to come here. Grandma Morgan, to him, was scarier than his mom could be. "She'll be calm and threatening at the same time."

"I don't know that something like that is possible." Dad laughed and turned when Grandma Morgan joined them in the forest. She was telling dad about the plum trees that she had picked this morning and how much she still disliked them. She looked at him. "So, young man, you ready to tell on those little bastards that are hurting you? I hope so. The entire forest is ready to go to battle for you."

"I never thought of them telling on me." She said that they loved him too and wanted to protect him. "I'll have to thank them for that. These kids, I don't want them killed off. You understand that, right, grandma?"

She pretended to think about it and then tickled him. Never in his life had he been tickled like his grandma did it. It was the most comforting thing in the world to him. To laugh with his grandma. When she promised him that she'd not kill anyone off, he felt a great deal better.

"While we're talking about things, I was wondering if you could get the lad into a better school. Not on account of the bullies, though. I hate that most of all, but he's struggling with the classes because of him being so smart." He'd never told anyone but Thad that he was smarter than his teachers. And Mrs. Mann knew it too. That's why she hated him so much. "I feel his teacher is intimidated by him and encourages the bullying when he outdoes the other kids on tests. Not a good environment if you ask me for studying."

"No, I'd think not." Grandma looked at him, and so did his dad. "Why haven't you told us that you're too smart for the classroom? We could have gotten you into something else."

"I can't protect my sisters if you did that." Sammy looked away, then back at his dad. A look of protective determination was etched on his young features. "I can't let them be targets in school. Just being related to me, they get some of the kids making fun of them. If I leave, they might hurt them. I'd never be able to live with myself if anything happened to Wendy and Bethy."

"I'll talk to your mom." Sammy thanked his dad. "You will stay focused on studying no matter how much they get into your face, all right?"

"I will, Dad." When they left them, Sammy laid back against the tree again. The song was different this time, and he found it relaxing him quicker. Knowing that Thad could stay and that his bullying situation at school was being taken care of had taken a huge weight off his shoulders. Just as he was dozing off, it hit him on how to make the water go where he wanted it to. Standing up, he used his considerable magic and made it snake its way to where he needed it to go. In just a few minutes, the water was flowing to the little plants, and the faeries were happy. Sitting back down, Thad laughed.

"It helps when you can clear the mind, sometimes, doesn't it?" He smiled at his friend and told him sometimes it does. "I'm glad I'm going to be around, Sammy. Just to see you growing with the magic. I'm thrilled beyond words to be your friend, but I'm thinking you need to hang out with people your own age. Just for some fun."

"All right. I will." Closing his eyes again, he smiled. "I was going to tell you to hang out with people your own age, too, but I think that you'd look silly talking to dirt and rocks."

They both laughed at that. Even as Sammy sat there, his mind was never stopping. Not only did he fix other things with the magic that he had, but he thought up ways to make other things work around the world. But there were no more thoughts of bullies. No more him worrying about his sisters. He was nearly asleep when he made up a way for the bees to pollinate some of the plants faster. Sammy was enjoying being a part of something so grand, and he was going to do his very best to make sure that he took care of everything that he could daily too.

~*~

Leslie had asked for the entire day off to deal with this trouble that his kids were having. Mom had wanted to go, but like Sammy, he was afraid that she'd zap a few people into the next month, and that wouldn't have been good for anyone. But he told her he'd call her if he needed her. She said she was going to hold him to that.

Even after talking to Wendy, he found out that

she, too, was being bullied for being smart. Since Bethy was too young to be in school yet, he knew that she was safe from harm. For now, anyway. That's why he wanted to get this finished up before she entered school, and it was still going on. However, Leslie was about as pissed off as he'd ever been about Sammy and Wendy's situations.

Mrs. Mann, along with Mr. Beck, the principal, came into the room with them. There were two other couples in the room with he and Veni, but he didn't know them, so he ignored them for now. It wasn't until Mrs. Mann called on one of the people behind him that he understood these were the parents of the kids his children were having trouble with. Veni stood up.

"Stay in your seat, Mr. Caulker. Or I'll put you back in it. I'm not in the mood to hear from anyone else at the moment." Veni looked at the teacher before speaking again. "You are not in charge of the meeting. We are. We called it and worked to get everyone here. I haven't any idea why either one of you thought it would be necessary to have the accused parents here, but we'll handle that as well." The man called Mr. Caulker started yelling.

"Accused? What are you talking about? I'm here to file a complaint against that monster of a kid of yours. He's been knocking the crap out of my boys since he was put in the classroom. If not for Mrs. Mann's help, we might not have known the extent of the problem your kid is causing." Leslie stood up when the man took a step in the direction of his wife. "You think you're a big man with all the money, don't you? Well, I'm not going to sit back and allow your monsters to kill one of my kids because he thinks he's so much smarter than them."

"He *is* smarter than them. Mrs. Mann, too, so I'm thinking that's been the issue with her. But how about if we have a look at some neighborhood cameras that I've been told about. These are from the houses along the walkway that my son takes home." He opened his computer and let them see where Mr. Caulker's sons were throwing rocks and sticks at Sammy. "As you can see here, this is where it gets really nasty. Also, if you look right here, you'll see

Mrs. Mann and Mr. Beck encouraging the other boys by handing them sticks and other things to throw at my son."

They watched each of the houses' recordings as Sammy tried to run from them. Even when he was down, the three boys kicked Sammy until Mrs. Mann called them off. He wished there was sound on the recording. He knew what Mrs. Mann had said to the boys because of Veni. She told the boys that they didn't need to kill him just yet. That sent chills down his spine each time he thought about the cold way that she had said it.

"How do we know you didn't doctor that up? You have the money for it. I know how you work things out in your favor. Mrs. Mann told us how you got your son out of other trouble too." Leslie showed them the time and date stamp on the recording. He handed all of them an affidavit from the police department about how they had reviewed the recordings and had found them to be legitimate and not messed with. He read it over before sitting back in his chair. "Christ, this is not what I've been told."

"I don't doubt that at all. However, as you can see, your boys are the ones that are doing this to my son." Mr. Caulker said that he'd been misled. About everything. "Yes, I can see that as well. The thing is, now, we have to figure out how to make this stop and that the boys aren't going to do this again."

"They won't. I promise you on that." Veni asked if he was going to beat them. "Yes. I have to show them that this isn't the way to treat people."

"That's up to you. But I think you should think about how you're using violence to stop violence. I'm not saying not to punish them. Never that. They need to be punished. However, whipping them is about the same as they're doing too. I think, and this is just me, that we should take care of the source of the problem. And I think that you'll agree when you say that it's these two and find out why your sons and the others are doing this. It might be simply because they had no choice in the matter. I'm not telling you what to do, Mr. Chalker. But there has to be a reason why these two were there to encourage the boys to do what they were doing." Mrs. Mann stood up.

"You're a liar. I knew that you'd come in here and try to say that I was part of your kid being a little shit. He is forever undermining me when he *thinks* that I'm wrong. I'm not. Not ever. If you think this is going to get me fired, then you're off your rocker. I've been a teacher here for the last twenty years, and I'm not going to be pushed aside because, in my otherwise boring job, I wanted to have a little fun. The board will never agree to anything against me and Mr. Beck here." Leslie pointed to the camera on the wall and said that they'd been listening all along. "You can't record me without my permission. I'll sue you for this. This is, it's slander."

"It's not slander if it's true." Leslie stood up just as the police were let into the room. "I'm pressing charges against the two of you for causing harm to my son and daughter, Wendy and Samuel Golden. Mr. Caulker, would you like to press charges as well?"

"Yes, I do. I believe that the two of you should be charged with bullying too. I don't have any idea what you might have said to my boys, but I'm telling you right now that it's going to get your asses in trouble for a long time." He put out his hand to him, and Leslie took it with his own. "I can't thank you enough for what you've done here today. It could have been a good deal worse than it turned out, and I can't thank you enough for your help in this."

Inviting the others out to lunch with them, Leslie was glad that the other parents were supportive. Not only that, but they were going to add to the charges against the teacher and principal about things that they had only just learned about this morning by telling their children where they were going. Things were looking good for a change, and Leslie was glad that he'd been able to talk to his son and daughter. Without the help of Thad, he did wonder how much longer it might have gone on.

On their way home, they decided that they needed to get a start on their home. The faeries were willing to help with anything that they needed, but Veni thought it would be more fun for them if they were able to pick out what they wanted for their rooms.

Wendy had purchased herself a computer, and while she'd been at it, she'd gotten one for Sammy as well. The two of them were taking online college classes that he didn't know about and were doing very well with them. Leslie needed to spend more time with his kids so that he could keep up with what they did all the time. He couldn't have been more proud of them than he was today.

"I think that we should get us a hotel room for the night and take them out to dinner. All three of them." He loved that idea. "Also, you should invite your mom and Tom too. They've been really good about letting us handle this with the kids, and they should be rewarded for it."

"I'm not going to tell my mom that. You can, but I'm not." They both laughed. "I have to admit I was only just thinking about how much I've been missing with me working all the time. I need to cut my day down to a few hours in the evening so that I can spend some time with them. I know I'll have a lot of fun with that. Especially with Thanksgiving coming up and then Christmas. Oh. Before I forget,

Scout and Allison are coming home in a couple of days. The work they were doing overseas has come to an end, and I think they're just excited to be coming home."

When they arrived home, at the home they were sharing with their family, they rode the horse and buggy over to the new place and let the kids pick out their rooms. It would be strange to live in a home all by himself with his new family, but he thought that their mom was right. It was time to branch out. Also, he loved the idea that they could see to more of the land by being out where they could see it all now.

Mom couldn't join them as she was going to have dinner with Tom and his children tonight to see if they could ask them to build on the land as well. They were already becoming vital to the works on the land, and with Susan, Tom's only daughter, knowledge of shipping, they were making headway on getting things that were needed, building material and such delivered in a timely manner too. It would be used to build or repair homes in town that needed a serious overhaul.

After picking out her bedroom, Wendy approached her dad. "Dad, is there going to be any trouble at school? Mom didn't kill anyone, did she? I watched the news, and they didn't mention it." He picked Wendy up and hugged her after telling her that her mom had been amazing. "Well, she's always amazing. And Aunt Sin is going to help me with some of the dresses that I like. She is going to give us all blankets as housewarming gifts too. I've seen mine. It's all girly with pink and purple. I can't wait until I have a bed to put it on."

"I'm excited too about them. She's going to be able to keep a lot of people warm this winter and beyond. Also, the faeries are excited to have some of the material for their homes as well. They'd do just about anything for Sin since she was so nice to give them her bits of material." Wendy told him how she'd gotten some of it, too and was going to make a doll with it for Bethy for Christmas. "You know, that's a good idea. We'll all make our gifts for one another like we usually do. I love that you're thinking of your sister too."

As they were going into Columbus, he didn't drive so that he could talk to the kids. They were a good deal smarter than he thought they were. Even Bethy, who was just beginning to talk, was saying things to him that he was enjoying.

By the time they were settled in their hotel rooms, he was almost too excited to go to dinner. He wanted to take them out shopping and let them have fun. Not that they didn't have fun anyway, but he wanted to be there firsthand when they shopped. He had never enjoyed being away from the compound as he was right at this moment.

"You need to calm the fuck down." He looked at Veni. "You're acting all giddy and stuff, and they're not used to it. You're freaking them out."

"I guess I might be. But I want to enjoy them so much today." She asked him if something was going to happen to them if he didn't do it right now. "No. I guess not. But I've never been able to do this with them before."

"Yes, you have. You've been too busy. I'm glad that you're going to be cutting down on your work to be at home more. I think they'll enjoy it. I know that I will." He rubbed her belly where their children were resting. "I want too much for them, but I don't want them to be horrible little shits either. Moderation."

"Yeah, right." She told him that she was serious. "I am too. I don't think that spoiling them once in a while is going to make them into little shits. My mom would murder me if I tried that. But once in a while, we can have some fun by letting them go a little wild. Especially since I missed them being hurt."

"We both missed that. But you're right. I guess it won't hurt for them to have a bit of fun once in a while." Once they were settled and cleaned up, lunch was going to be a priority. Not only were they going to have lunch, but they were considering going to a movie as well. Leslie wasn't so sure about taking Bethy to a movie, but they'd cross that bridge later. They had food to eat and stores to conquer. He was going to have so much fun.

Chapter 7

Scout wasn't sure what was going on at the airport where they were, but he did reach out beyond where they were sitting to see if he had anything to worry about. All he found out was that the police were looking for a man and woman posing as elderly people and were considered armed and dangerous. Asking Allison if she'd sit on his other side, he was glad when she wasn't on the end seat and between a wall and him. He saw the couple in question just as he was reaching out again.

After telling Allison about what was going on, she started searching the area too. They both spotted the couple at the same time. They were stripping off the clothing that deemed them elderly and now appeared to be a couple in their early to mid-twenties.

"What do we do?" He said that he didn't know but didn't want to get involved unless they had to. "Well, I'm thinking that if they get out of this airport, it's going to be a danger to the people outside of here. Especially if it comes to a shoot-off or something."

"I didn't think of that." She told him that was why she was the brains of the two of them. Scout laughed. "Good thinking. So, what is your plan, brainy?"

He had fallen in love with her the moment that he'd met her. She was bright, funny and didn't take things overly seriously. Nothing like him. Scout was usually the one that saw the dark side of everything and that he didn't have a sense of humor. Not even a little one. However, he could feel himself getting better at teasing her daily, and that was good for them both.

"The man is armed. I think the woman is as well, but I can't tell from here." When Allison stood up, he asked her where she was going. "To the ladies' room to disarm her if she is armed. I think that you should go to the men's room and see what you can do about the man. Even if we only detain them long enough for the police to get here, that'll save some others from getting harmed."

"I agree, but I don't like it." She kissed him on the mouth and told him he was a good player. "Allison, don't get hurt. I know that you're this badass phoenix and all, but you can still be hurt."

"So can you. Just do what you've been practicing with me, and we'll both be fine. It'll be a piece of cake, you'll see." He no more believed that they'd not be hurt than he did that this would be a piece of cake. It was dangerous for them both."

Getting up to go to the men's room, the man was standing at the urinal. Scout didn't want to stand next to him with his dick out, so he entered the bathroom and closed the door. Putting his hand on the wall where the man had been standing, Scout heated up the wall to the point where he could hear the water boiling out of the commodes and urinal. When the man screamed, Scout stepped out of the stall and touched his shoulder with his finger.

He knew that it had to hurt him. Scout had been able to cook a chicken with his fingers after heating them up. While it didn't seem like a very useful thing, being able to cook a chicken with his finger, it had been a very tasty meal.

Hitting the man in the face when he jumped back from him, Scout turned on the cold water to cool his hands down. It would have eventually cooled off enough, but he needed it done quickly. The burn on the man's shoulder would heal, but he'd be fucking sore for some time to come.

Calling for the police, he told them that he'd only just come across the man on the floor when he'd entered. After a couple of more questions, the police were headed to the ladies' room. Allison said that the woman on the floor had tried to take her car keys, a good story, he thought, and she'd had to rough her up. They both went back to their seats after taking the memory from the police officer's mind about them and waiting on their connecting flight.

"I can't wait to get back home." He told Allison that he was thinking the same thing. "To see your family again is going to be wonderful, but I'm looking forward to a homecooked meal that isn't going to kill me if I eat it. Some of the food we were being served was questionable, don't you think?"

"I'm just happy that you have the thought of cooking it more so that any bacteria was gone. Some of the chicken wasn't quite to my liking the way it was pink inside." She agreed with him. "The thing that I'm enjoying most about this heating shit up magic is the way I can have a nice hot cup of tea whenever I want it. It's wonderful not to have to wait on the water to boil."

"I noticed that about you too. You didn't much care for the tea when you had it." He told her that it wasn't his mom's special brew. "I guess that makes sense. While I've never had it, the way that you go on about it makes me want a cup of it right now."

They were good at having conversations. About

everything. They were also very good at enjoying the silence. Sometimes they could sit and read or watch something on the television for hours and not say a word. But once they were on a subject, they could go on for a few days about whatever it was they were talking about. Like the menu at the restaurant they'd eaten at several days ago.

The food had been all right, nothing that spectacular. It filled the void was about all he could say about it. But the décor in the room was amazing. There were things on every inch of the walls that reminded him of the country they were in. Allison had enjoyed the plants, all different varieties of them, that they'd asked their faeries, Bobo and Peanut, to see if these plants were something that they could grow at home. They both took very small cuttings from the ones that they had liked, which was nearly all of them and said they'd work on them when they got back home. That was another thing that he was excited about too. Telling his family how well things went.

They had had some issues at first. But once the

local cops figured out that he nor Allison were going to back down from them, the hospital was up and running in a few weeks. Even the naysayers were lining up to get checked out for cuts and illnesses that the hospital could take care of. Scout was happy that he'd got to do this work with Allison. She was like a breath of spring air to him.

"Once we're on the second flight, you'll call your mom?" He said that he'd been talking to her all along. "Me too. She's been keeping me updated on the things going on around the place. I hurt for Sammy and Wendy, but I'm glad that they were able to get it taken care of so easily."

"I am as well. What do you think about having our own home when we return?" She said that she'd never owned a home before, so she couldn't wait to put her stamp on one. "Good. I was hoping you'd be the one that did the decorating. My rooms at my mom's house still have boxes that I brought home from college the last time I was there. I don't remember the last time I made my bed either."

"I usually just throw a blanket over mine when

I get up and move on. Sleeping in a sleeping bag all this time makes me think that I'll never do that again. I want a nice mattress under me with lots of soft blankets over me. I guess it's getting colder at home." He told her that they'd had several dustings of snow since they'd been gone. "I don't have a lot of snow memories in my life. Once it started to get really cold, my family would move to where it was warm. Then when they stayed in Florida, I didn't leave there much either. I'm sure I'll get used to it in no time."

"I know that we, as leopards, love the colder months. With all our fur, it's nice to be able to play in the cold weather and snow." He'd forgotten how much fun they had in the winter months. It had been a long time since any of them had made the time to do anything like that. He was going to make sure that they did this winter. Even if he had to drag them out kicking and screaming.

As they were seated on their last flight. The two of them leaned back to sleep. This wasn't the longest leg of their journey, but it was going to be the most exhausting. They'd been in planes for the past four days to get home, and he thought he could rest for a week. While he didn't sleep anymore, he still needed his rest.

Allison curled her body around his and laid her head on his chest. They'd been traveling as husband and wife since they'd left home, and he couldn't wait to make that a reality. She'd not told him yet that she loved him. Scout couldn't have been more in love with Allison than he was with his own mom. She was so very special to him.

While she slept, he reached out to his mom. Telling her about the incident at the airport, he was glad that she wasn't overly upset about it. She told him how the issue with the kids was resolved, and he was glad they had such a great role model as their father.

"I've been looking at some of the things that are in the big barn here. There is a great deal of furniture that I think I'll have the faeries clean up for me. If you don't want it, the others have turned it down, I think I'm going to auction it off. There are quite a few items in there that

have been out there since you boys were babies. I don't know that anyone would want that, either. It's extremely old and chewed up. You guys teethed on anything that was wood."

"Yes, I remember that." He laughed a little. *"I don't know that I'd want it either, but I'll ask Allison if she wants to have a look at it. I've been meaning to tell you about things that I discovered about over here. There are a lot of families that are going without for basic needs. When I tracked down where they could get them, I was told that the police and the rest of the government take what they wanted first, then leaves the rest for the town. I began reproducing things for them so that they'd not run out, but that won't help them if someone finds out."*

"We'll work on that when you get back. How are the gardens going? I'm assuming that they're being raided as well. People in power taking the lion's share first?" He told her that is what it looked like. Then he laughed as he told her what he'd found out too. *"So they're making two gardens and not working too hard on the one that the police can see. I love that idea. I hope you were able to help them out with that."*

"*Of course I did. They're getting a nice bounty now. Allison and I showed them how to dry the things they're putting away for themselves too. And the water that runs by here, I made sure that the animals around the area knew that we were trying to protect the people there, and they said that they'd not bother the things they've had in the water to keep hidden. Also, I spoke to the local gnomes there, and they're going to keep an eye on other things that the people can put away for their families. It's bad but not as bad as I've seen it, Mom.*" She told him how proud she was of him for working with the other creatures. "*Speaking of which, Sammy has been speaking to the trees around this sort of area. The trees are making sure that the secondary gardens are protected from the poachers as well as they're making sure that they get plenty of sun for the gardens too. That kid has far-reaching magic. I'll say that for him.*"

They spoke for another hour, and he felt better about what they were planning to do. While Scout didn't think of himself as a momma boy, he was very close to her. He had been talking to his mom about things that were going on around the hospital and was glad that she was on board with the things that he'd been able to do to help out. He'd yet to tell her about him being just as much a phoenix as Allison was.

The flight wasn't that bad. The weather was good, so they didn't have any turbulence while flying. Allison woke up twice. Once when he needed to move, but she went back to sleep almost immediately. Then when she'd had to go to the bathroom. She returned with a smile on her face and seemed to be more rested than he'd seen her be in the last month.

"I want a cheeseburger when I get home." He closed his hand around hers, and she squealed in delight when a burger appeared there. As she ate her burger, he handed her fries as well as a milkshake to go with it. She ate every bite of it too. "Why didn't you do that for me before?"

"You never requested anything before. Well, but for a shower. Which, if you remember, I did help you find a way to get one of those too." She glared at him. "Didn't you get clean? I mean, it was a shower."

"It was a bag of water hanging from a tree. You heated it up nicely, but it was far from a shower. I did get cleaned up, though. I thank you for that." They were both laughing when the stewardess came by to ask if they needed anything. After giving them both a bottle of water, she went on her way. The two of them were sick of that too. Bottled water. He wanted a glass of cold water in a glass filled with ice.

They were still another hour from the Columbus airport when Allison fell asleep again. It had been a very exhausting trip, and he was glad that she was getting rested up as much as she could. She wasn't to the point yet where she didn't need to sleep. Of course, if they were to make love, she'd have all the powers that he did. And he'd have what she was as well.

Scout was glad that they were going to be met at the airport by his brother. Marley and his family were there to do some shopping, and it just so happened that the hotel they were staying in had room for them to stay a few more days to wait on him and Allison. He could do with a few days of people being around him. And was glad that Carroll didn't mind changing his plans to pick him up. A few more hours and they'd be home. He couldn't wait.

~*~

Marley was doing a walk-through when he realized that he wasn't alone in the big house. All kids had stayed home from school today until things were straightened out there, and he was glad it was being taken care of. The little boy in front of him looked a good deal like one of the ones from the recorders where Sammy had been hurt.

"I know that you're a Golden, but I don't know which one." He told him that he was Marley, the doctor. "I thought so. My momma said that you helped her once when she'd fallen down the stairs at work. Then one of the others had helped her get money from the place. Is that right? Oh, I'm Sherman Clark. Everyone just calls me Shermie."

"Hello, Shermie. Yes, I remember your mom being hurt and my brother Shiloh helping her with the business she worked for. Is everyone all right?" Shermie nodded but didn't look him in the eye. "I was just trying to figure out which room is which when you came around. I know where the kitchen is but not—"

"My brother is hurting bad." Marley, ready to go and help the kid waited when Shermie put up his hand to stop him. "He's dying. Gilbert is his name. He's got luck-u-me or something like that."

"Leukemia?" Shermie nodded. "I'm sorry to hear that, Shermie. I had no idea that there was anyone sick in your family. Has he been fighting it for very long?"

"I don't know. But momma, she's really upset that he's going to die. Me too, but I sure hate to see my momma crying. It hurts me way deep in my chest area." He told him that it did him, too, when his mom did the same thing. Marley made his way to the little boy and sat next to him on what would be their front porch. "I got it, too, I guess. I don't want to make my momma suffer any more than she is right now, but she will. I know it."

It hurt Marley that a child would die from something like the boy had. It hurt him twice as badly that there were two of them from the same family. Reaching out to touch the boy's arm, he could see that he was indeed dying from the disease but that he'd been bedbound like his brother soon. Healing the boy caused him no harm, and he was glad to have done it when he looked up at him.

"You did something to me." He said that he did. "Can you do that same for Gilbert? He's my little brother, and I don't want him to die either."

"I'd have to see him first. It might be too late for me to save him. Sometimes the disease can do more harm once it's set in the body." They walked to Shermie's home. Even before they were in the house, he could feel all the sickness in the home. Not only were the children sick, the other boy and a little girl but so was the mister of the family. The mother was the only one that wasn't ill with leukemia, but she was exhausted from caring for the family.

"Mom, I need you at the Clark home. As soon as possible. Have the faeries come with fruit and juices too. Also, get one of the blankets that Sin made, please. It'll be something that we can wrap a body in before the police

arrive." She didn't ask him any questions, only to ask him how many there were. *"Two children that are left, a father who won't make it too much longer and a mother who is trying her best to make them all live. Hurry."*

The younger boy had died before he'd arrived. Shermie's mother had been sitting out on the porch sobbing. Even as his mom showed up with food and drinks for the little family, the father passed away as well. Getting the little girl healthy was a priority for him, and Shermie helped by making sure that his mom had plenty to eat and drink.

After healing Carolynn, the little girl's mom took Shermie and her to her home. They'd be well cared for, better than they'd get at any hospital because of the magic mom had. Calling the police, Sin showed up with the blankets to wrap the little boy in but didn't with the older man. He was too large, and moving him around could harm her with his weight. After she left him, taking blankets to the other people in the household, Marley set about figuring out how the household had gone so long without help.

He found the reason out almost immediately

by touching the dead man. The father was much too proud, and since he had been the carrier for the cancer, he wouldn't allow his wife to get help. Just in the event that he would be blamed for the deaths that he was sure were coming. Marley wanted to knock the man around a bit so that he'd understand that he'd effectively nearly killed off his entire family, including his poor wife.

After the police left the home and the bodies were removed, he went to the hospital to see to Mrs. Clark. He'd ordered tests on her as well as set her up with an IV and to make sure that she was resting. She was sleeping when he arrived, and he left more orders for her when he got the blood test results back. Christ, it was a small wonder that any of them were able to get around. She was not just malnourished but dehydrated as well. After checking on her again, he left for home. Mom was feeding the other two children when he got there.

"Your momma sure does make a good pancake, Doctor Marley." He said that he knew that, and her jelly was great too. "I know. I had some grape, and

Carolynn had some of her cherry. We've not had good food like this for a while."

He watched them eating as he sat down with them. Mom handed him a plate of pancakes, but he declined them. His heart was hurting too badly right now. Understanding, mom put the pancakes on the kids' plates, much to their happiness. Marley asked Shermie why he'd come to find him. He put his fork down, and Marley wanted to tell him that he was sorry he asked.

"I knew that my brother was gone already. I didn't tell momma yet but went to find us some help. My daddy, he was cussing at me about leaving the house, but I knew that my momma was going to be next if I didn't get her any help. I already figured that I was a goner and wanted to make sure that she was all right." He told him that his mother was in the hospital for a few days to get some rest and food in her belly. "She was so busy all the time making sure that Gilbert and us were getting food, but she never took time for herself. I didn't care that my daddy was going to die. He was mean all the time anyway to momma. But you saved me, too and Carolynn. I'll never be able to thank you for that in a million years."

"You just get better, and that will be payment enough, Shermie." He played around with his food for a few seconds, then looked up at him. "You can tell me anything you need to, Shermie. My family and I are going to make sure that you and the rest of your family are all right."

"My daddy burned up the money that my momma got from falling down. She told him that she could have used it for the doctor bills. But he told her that he was the man of the family and that he'd decide where the money went. So he went and burned it all up one day." Marley was having a difficult time holding onto his temper about Mr. Clark. It wasn't until Sin put her hand on his shoulder that he was able to calm down. "When he was first sick, momma had to wait on him, foot and board. The doctor told him that he needed to lose some weight and to exercise. Then they found out that he was sick with blood cancer."

"Diabetes." It was Carolynn that told him that

was it. "Then they found out he had leukemia, and he didn't try to get better, I'm betting."

"The money was all gone by then." Carolynn looked at her brother before continuing. "Me and my brothers, we tried to get some money coming in. Collecting cans and bottles to have turned in. We even tried to steal some apples from your orchard, Mrs. Morgan, but it was too heavy for us to carry the basket once we filled it. It wasn't until I come down with something that we realized that we all were going to die. But we didn't stop trying to help momma. She was getting sicker than all of us by waiting on dad all the time."

"I'll make sure you have all the fruit you need when your mom is better." It was Shermie who asked if their mom was going to get better. "She will. My son is a good doctor, and he'll take care that she's well. Once she's up and about, we'll make sure that you have food in your home and bellies as well as anything else you might need."

After getting the children bathed and in one of his old shirts each, they were put in beds from his room. They were asleep in no time. A full belly and less worry would do that for a child, he knew. Sitting in the kitchen with his mom and Tom, Marley did something that he'd never done before, he cried over the loss of a patient.

"He was only fourteen years old. Shermie is ten, and Carolynn is twelve. That's too young for them to be losing a brother. My heart hurts for them and their mother." She told him that they'd take care that they were all right. "I know but that father should have watched out for his family first and foremost, don't you think?"

"You might not want to hear this, but the mother should have been a little more proactive. Not waiting on that grown man would have been the first thing I would have done." Sin agreed with her. "However, we don't know the circumstances, so we can only speculate on how things were in there. Listening to a version of a child isn't going to get us all the answers. How is the mother? She going to make it?"

"Yes. She's going to need some rest for a few

weeks. I don't mean that she has to be in the hospital for that long, but she's going to need someone to come in and help her around the house until she's better." Mom nodded. "I know that this sounds horrible, but I don't find myself wanting to be very generous towards her. All three of those kids would have died had Shermie not found me."

"Like I said, we don't know what went on there. I'm not saying that I'm feeling any more generous about helping them, but there might have been something else that was going on that we're not privy to." Mom patted him on the back as she went to the sink. "I'm going to make a big dinner tomorrow night. I'd very much like it if you all were able to come. We need some comfort food, I'm thinking."

He agreed with her and then suggested that they have a roasted pig to feast on. Since Sin had never had anything like that, she was excited to give it a shot. Even his brothers seemed like it was the best idea ever and started making plans on making it happen. He thought about his brother Scout and wondered if Allison could help them along with it but decided that he wasn't going to bring it up. He was just happy that they were all getting together.

After going back to his home with Sin, they talked about their home. It was bigger than he'd thought when he told the faeries what they wanted, but he was very pleased with it. They were going to sleep in it tonight and was glad that the faeries had seen to the bedroom and made sure that it was ready for them. As soon as he walked into the room, he couldn't have been more pleased.

All three sides that were on the outside of the room were floor to ceiling windows. No carpets on the floor, which were all hardwood. The large shower in the bathroom meant that he and Sin could shower together, and he was in love with the fireplace in the bedroom. He might never leave the room once he got into bed.

The rest of the house was just as beautiful. They'd toured the living room with another fireplace in it. There were two offices that were connected that they could share. The kitchen, while not his domain, was big enough for hanging out while the food was being cooked, and he thought that it was modeled after his mom's.

They didn't bother with the other bedrooms. They were, he knew, emptied until they were needed. But having a home of his own to share with the love of his life was something that he'd never given any thought to. Now that he had it, Marley didn't want to have to ever go back to sharing again. While he loved his mom, this was the way that it should be when you had a family to raise.

Before You Go...

HELP AN AUTHOR

write a review

THANK YOU!

Share your voice and help guide other readers to these wonderful books. Even if it's only a line or two, your reviews help readers discover the author's books so they can continue creating stories that you'll love. Log in to your favorite retailer and leave a review. Thank you.

AWARD WINNING, BESTSELLING AUTHOR

Kathi Barton, a winner of the Pinnacle Book Achievement award as well as a best-selling author on Amazon and All Romance books, lives in Nashport, Ohio, with her husband, Paul. When not creating new worlds and romance, Kathi and her husband enjoy camping and going to auctions. She can also be seen at county fairs with her husband, who is an artist and potter.

Her muse, a cross between Jimmy Stewart and Hugh Jackman, brings her stories to life for her readers in a way that has them coming back time and again for more. Her favorite genre is paranormal romance, with a great deal of spice. You can visit Kathi on line and drop her an email if you'd like. She loves hearing from her fans. aaronskiss@gmail.com.

Follow Kathi on her blog: http://kathisbartonauthor.blogspot.com/